# The Yellow Sock

an adoption story

Angela Hunt

# DEDICATION

For Taryn and Tyler, who are and always will be
my "trees of life . . ."

With special thanks to Dr. Lisa Mallett, D.V.M,
Seminole, Florida

Selected Books by Angela Hunt

*Roanoke*
*Jamestown*
*Hartford*
*Rehoboth*
*Charles Towne*
*Magdalene*
*The Novelist*
*Uncharted*
*The Awakening*
*The Debt*
*The Elevator*
*The Face*
*Let Darkness Come*
*Unspoken*
*The Justice*
*The Note*
*The Immortal*
*The Truth Teller*
*The Silver Sword*
*The Golden Cross*
*The Velvet Shadow*
*The Emerald Isle*
*Dreamers*
*Brothers*
*Journey*
*Doesn't She Look Natural?*
*She Always Wore Red*
*She's In a Better Place*

Web page: www.angelahuntbooks.com

# ONE

"Mrs. Leber?" Megan Wingfield looked up from the medical chart in her hand and smiled at the petite woman sitting on the edge of a chair in the examination room. "I've got some interesting news for you. Princess is not sick or overweight—she's pregnant. Carrying five puppies, to be exact, and due in about a week."

"Pregnant?" The older woman's face went pale. "Impossible. Princess stays in the house with me except when I go to work, and then she's in a fenced back yard. She hasn't been around any other dogs."

Megan lifted a brow. "Any holes under your fence? Any loose boards? You'd be surprised how easy it is for a determined dog to, er, visit."

The woman shook her head decisively. "It's a chain link fence, and I keep my yard locked up tight as a drum. No way Princess has had a visitor."

Megan folded her arms. "Well, she's definitely pregnant, so there's a daddy dog somewhere in your neighborhood. You might begin by asking your neighbors if their male dogs have been neutered."

"Oh, my." If possible, Mrs. Leber's face went a shade paler. "My precious purebred . . ."

"Great Danes are wonderful dogs," Megan said, trying to soften the blow, "so even if the puppies are mixed, they are sure to inherit many of Princess' fine qualities."

"You don't understand." The red line of Mrs. Leber's mouth thinned for a moment, and her throat tightened as she swallowed. "That annoying boy who lives behind me—he has

1

a male dog. A Chihuahua. A yappy, irritating, pesky little runt that is always yipping at Princess through the fence . . ."

In spite of herself, Megan grinned. A Chihuahua could easily slip beneath a chain link fence, but she couldn't imagine what sort of pups would result from a union between a giant, docile Dane and a high-strung toy breed.

"We'll have to see what the puppies are like when they are born." Megan moved toward the door. "Now, if you'll excuse me a moment, I'll go get Princess. The doctor will be in to discuss the delivery with you."

"Five puppies," Mrs. Leber murmured, her gaze drifting toward the wall. "What am I supposed to do with five bizarre little mutts?"

After closing the door behind her, Megan walked back to the x-ray room, where Dr. Bob Duncan and Tom, another technician, were easing the huge Harlequin Dane off the examination table. Princess was a sweet animal, though in her present condition she seemed all legs and belly.

"Mrs. Leber thinks the pups might have been fathered by a Chihuahua," Megan told the doctor, trying her best not to giggle.

"Egads." Dr. Duncan's genial face split into a grin. "Won't that be an interesting combination?"

The black and white Dane lumbered over to Megan and sniffed at her fingers.

"You want a treat?" Megan pulled the bottle of canine vitamins from her pocket and opened it. "You're a lucky girl. You get two—one for you, and one for the pups."

"Is she going to be all right?" Dr. Duncan asked, turning toward the door.

Megan flashed him a wry smile. "Mrs. Leber or Princess?"

The doctor laughed. "I know the dog will be fine. I'm worried about the owner."

"I think she'll be okay once she gets over the shock," Megan said, slipping her hand beneath the huge dog's collar. "But we might have to help her find homes for those puppies."

"Hmmm." The doctor made a polite sound as he took the dog's chart and scribbled a note. "Ought to insist upon spay/neuters for the pups, too, as soon as possible. I don't think I'd want to encourage the breeding of Great Chihuahuas."

"No, sir."

Following the doctor, Megan led the pregnant Princess to the examination room and paused as the doctor pasted on a straight face. After giving her a "here goes nothing" look, he opened the door and called out in a cheery voice, "Mrs. Leber! I hear you're about to become the grandmother of five!"

Megan lowered her head to hide her expression as she led the Great Dane into the exam room. The huge spotted dog had never found it easy to maneuver in the room designed more for cats and small breeds, so it took Megan a full five minutes to pull the heavily expectant animal into the open space between the patient door and the exam table.

As the doctor tried to explain why Mrs. Leber should build a whelping box no matter what breed had fathered the puppies, Megan urged Princess to sit. The gentle giant was eager to comply, and dropped to the cool tiles with a long sigh. Megan sat beside her on the floor. As she stroked the dog's neck, she felt her own thoughts drifting away.

Life. Birth. Death. Every day she saw the cycle repeated in this office where animals were born, grew through the stages of development, and finally died in their weeping owners' arms. Her love of life and animals had brought her to this veterinary hospital, and she'd willingly stay forever if not for her own desire to experience the cycle of life.

She wanted a baby. And, if God was merciful, she might have one on the way.

She lowered her head to gaze into the Dane's beautiful brown eyes.

"When did you know?" she whispered, fondling the dog's silky ears. "Did you know right away, or did you have to wait until you felt the puppies moving?"

3

Princess didn't answer, but when she lifted her head Megan could have sworn the dog was smiling.

Most teachers had summers off, but Dave had chosen to spend his July teaching a summer school class for Alta Vista high school students who'd flunked American history. Often he remained late to tutor kids who were having difficulty in the intensive class, but his car stood in the driveway when Megan arrived home. She snatched her keys out of the ignition, sailed through the front door, and found her handsome husband on the deck, a plate of raw hamburger patties in his hand.

"Hi, Chef Wingfield." She gave him a quick kiss, then stood back and nodded appreciatively at flaming grill. "Hmm, those burgers look good. But be sure they're done in the middle, okay?" She almost added that eating raw meat was bad for pregnant women, but then thought the better of it.

"Have I ever fed you a raw hamburger?" Dave's blue eyes twinkled over his shoulder as she moved to a deck chair. "They don't call me Chef-Boy-ar-Dave for nothing."

"Yeah, right." She sank into the seat and propped her feet on the edge of the vacant chair behind her husband. Though the sun had begun to lower toward the Virginia mountains in the west, the air was still warm and muggy.

She pushed her bangs off her damp forehead and smiled up at him. "Have a good day?"

"The kids were fine, no problems." Dave dropped the patties onto the grill, where they immediately began to sizzle. "Dr. Comfort called to talk to me about next year. Seems she's thinking about making it her *last* year. She wants to retire."

Megan stared at him, a tingle of excitement beginning to flow through her veins. Dr. Stella Comfort was Dave's boss at Valley View Elementary School, where he worked during the regular school year. "If she's retiring—"

"Yep, she wants me to take her place. She says she'll

4

recommend me to the school board even though I'd be the youngest principal in the county."

"That's *wonderful* news, honey." Megan beamed at him as she fanned her face with her hand. "I always knew you were the best, but this proves it."

Dave shrugged. "It means Dr. Comfort likes my work. I'd still have to convince the school board I could handle the job, and there are other assistant principals who'd kill to have that spot."

"But you've been at that school four years. The teachers know and respect you, and the parents have never had a bad word to say—"

"All the same, it's up to the school board." Turning, he winked at her. "But thanks for the vote of confidence."

"You're welcome." Megan crossed her legs at the ankle, wondering if the fluttering in her stomach was the result of hunger or something else. "I might have some other good news."

His brow lifted. "Not another pet, I hope."

"No, two cats are enough." She looked down at her hands as a sudden feeling of awkwardness overtook her. How many times had they replayed this conversation?

"I'm two days late."

His voice softened. "You've been late before."

"Yeah, but today, around lunchtime, I felt really queasy. Laurie says that's how she felt in the first month. She said she couldn't even stand the *sight* of food."

"Maybe you ate something you shouldn't have."

"I didn't eat. I skipped lunch."

When Dave didn't answer, she hurried to fill the silence. "And there are other signs, too. Breast tenderness. And I'm tired, really tired. So on the way home I stopped to pick up another test kit."

His eyes, when she looked up, were soft with sympathy. "I'd wait a day or two," he whispered, keeping his gaze on her while he absently patted the burgers with a pancake turner. "Save your money."

Megan's eyes filled with tears as he turned his attention back to the grill. Why couldn't he be optimistic? They'd been through so much together—twenty-two long months of the struggle to conceive a baby. Everyone said they just needed to relax, to trust in God's timing, to let themselves settle into married life. Well, they'd been married and settled for three years and still there was no baby. No pregnancy. Nothing but hope after hope, month after month, an endless roller coaster of rising optimism and falling dreams . . .

Megan's stomach gurgled as the scent of sizzling fat reached her nostrils. She placed a protective hand over her belly, then pulled herself out of the deep chair. "Yell at me when the burgers are done," she called as she left the porch. "I'm going in to cool off."

Once inside the house, she locked herself in the bathroom. A moment later she discovered that Dave had been right— she *should* have saved her money and not bought the pregnancy kit. This would be another month without a baby.

After dashing tears from her eyes, she opened the cupboard beneath the sink and fumbled for the box of tampons. She tried to tell herself it was no big deal, just another minor setback, but her pep talk did nothing to stem the hot tears stinging her eyes.

Dave pressed the flat blade of the metal pancake turner to the mound of ground beef on the grill and blinked as steam rose from the dripping fat. He'd heard the note of resentment in Megan's voice, and he knew his wife was nearing the limits of her endurance. She'd been remarkably patient in the face of frustration, but soon she'd be looking at him again with mute appeal in her blue eyes.

They both wanted a child, but Megan had been far more active than he in the pursuit of their goal. After their first anniversary, Megan brought up the topic of children, and he agreed—they had been blessed with a home, their marriage was stable, and they were mature enough to pursue parenthood. So they stopped using birth control and waited for God to bless them with a baby.

Now, two years later, they were still waiting.

To her credit, Megan didn't become anxious right away. The books she read assured them that no couple should consider themselves infertile until they'd been unable to conceive for an entire year, so she waited six months before taking the matter up with her gynecologist. At her annual physical, the doctor did a cursory examination and said everything looked normal. To appease her doubts, he sent Megan home with charts and instructions on how to determine the time of her ovulation—prime time for conception. For three months Megan began the day with a thermometer in her mouth, then recorded her waking temperature. On the days that the thermometer dipped a degree, she told Dave that they'd reached the Appointed Time.

Dave had never minded the act of intimacy between a husband and his wife, but Megan's no-nonsense tone on those days was anything but romantic. Still, if her efforts and record-keeping resulted in a baby, he figured it would all be worthwhile.

After a year of temperature-taking, Megan tossed out her tattered charts and turned her eagle eye on Dave. A man's fertility, she told him, could depend upon what type of underwear he wore, so he had to switch from briefs to boxers. Dave grumbled at bit at this, but the concession seemed small when he considered what she had endured with her thermometers and charts.

After six months of boxer shorts, Megan's gaze narrowed even further. "You need to see a urologist," she told him in a flat voice. "There's no sense in me taking drugs if . . ."

*The problem lies with you.* Megan had left her sentence unfinished, but Dave could hear the note of accusation in her tone.

Trouble was, a visit to the urologist was at the bottom of his list of Enjoyable Pursuits. The appointment was certain to be inconvenient, uncomfortable, and embarrassing. He'd never been to a urologist before, and he wasn't eager to establish a relationship with any doctor who worked . . . down there.

But as he carried the steaming burgers into the kitchen, he saw Megan's watery eyes and knew they'd failed again. Those eyes lifted to him in a silent plea, and he found himself whispering, "Okay, honey. I'll make an appointment."

One week later, amid the yipping and yapping of a litter of miniature Doberman puppies in the waiting room, Megan paused behind the reception desk and glanced at the clock. Dave's appointment with the doctor had been scheduled for nine o'clock that morning, and at lunch he'd called to say that the doctor would have results by three. He'd be back in the classroom by that time, but if Megan wanted to call and check on things . . .

She forced herself to concentrate on the woman behind the counter. Her Persian cat, an aloof creature named King Midas, had just had his teeth cleaned, and was definitely unhappy with the situation.

"Here's the doctor's report," she said, handing a copy of the kitty health report to the cat's solicitous owner. "King Midas should be fine, but he'll need to have those teeth cleaned at least once a year."

As the woman moved away, Midas scowled at Megan, who scowled back, then shifted her gaze to the clock above the desk. One o'clock. Two more hours before she would know anything.

"Laurie," she said, turning her back on the waiting patients, "I'm going to the back for a minute."

Craving a moment of silence and privacy, she moved into the restroom, the locked the door and leaned against it. The afternoon had crept by, each moment longer than the one preceding it. The morning had begun like all the others, but at the breakfast table she had opened her book of daily devotions and read an unusual challenge. "What is the thing you want most from God right now?" the writer had asked. "Are you willing to surrender that desire so God can work His will in your life?"

She had stared at the page in silence, feeling oddly betrayed. Someone had been reading her mind; the author obviously knew her deepest secret. The thing she wanted most in life was to become pregnant, and no, she wasn't willing to abandon that desire . . . not while there was even a slight chance that her dream might become a reality.

Did God ask such things of His children? She'd grown up believing that if you followed the principles of the Bible, God would grant the desires of your heart. And He knew her heart's desire was a baby.

She exhaled slowly, then lifted her chin and stared in the small bathroom mirror, bracing herself to face the waiting patients and their owners. If she kept busy, this afternoon would pass quickly.

She counted the minutes between one and two, her eyes gravitating to the clock between patients. At one-thirty she'd prayed the Dave's test results would be good; at two o'clock she amended her prayer. "Please, Father," she prayed in the quiet x-ray room. "Let Your will be done, but please end this uncertainty. I'd rather know there was absolutely no chance for us to have children than continue this emotional roller coaster ride."

No matter how bad the news might be, Megan found comfort in the thought that their waiting might soon end. By some miracle of modern medicine, perhaps this doctor could provide an answer . . . and a baby. But even if all he could give was a clear reason why they had failed, at least the months of disappointment would end.

She made a face as she glanced at the calendar. Dr. Comfort, Dave's boss at Valley View Elementary, was coming to the house tonight. Dave felt that she wanted to discuss his future away from the school, so Megan had planned a nice dinner—cranberry chicken, tossed salad, and her famous yeast rolls. Maybe, if she had time after work, she'd whip up a chocolate chess pie for dessert.

Two-thirty found her at the desk, explaining the doctor's instructions to Mrs. Wilt, whose dainty Pekinese had developed a urinary tract infection. After Mrs. Wilt pocketed the prescription, Megan offered a flavored vitamin to the petite Peke, who accepted it with delicate pleasure. "Take care now," Megan said, smiling them out the door. "The doctor will call in a few days to see how she's doing."

Three o'clock found Megan at the desk again, her hands on the counter, her attention a million miles away from her job. When the minute hand of the large clock over the desk shifted and creaked past the straight vertical position, she picked up the phone and punched in the number she'd scrawled on an appointment card.

After being passed from the receptionist to the doctor's private office, Megan waited on hold for about five minutes, then heard a male voice.

"Mrs. Wingfield?"

"Yes?"

As the doctor proceeded to speak in a flat monotone, Megan stared at the image of a sad-eyed Bassett pup on the desk calendar. When he finished, she thanked him and hung up.

So that settled the matter. Her prayer had been completely answered in an instant. God didn't even want to negotiate.

She blinked as the image of the puppy began to waver. "Laurie," she said, turning toward the receptionist sitting behind her, "would you tell Dr. Duncan that I needed to leave early? It's sort of a family crisis."

Laurie opened her mouth as if to ask for details, then nodded wordlessly when she saw Megan's face.

Megan moved through the waiting room toward the door, a little amazed that her arms and legs and hands could still function. How could they open doors and walk and unlock the car when her brain was numb and her heart breaking?

# TWO

An hour later, Megan lay on her bed, the pillow damp beneath her cheeks. The sense of numbness had carried her home, but the dam broke when she crossed the threshold of their bedroom. After the tears, dry sobs wracked her body for a brief interval, then faded away.

The tears did nothing to ease the pain. She had thought she'd feel better after a good cry, but this burden was far too heavy to be wept away in an hour.

Lying there, she listened to the steady click of the cuckoo clock in the hall and waited for the sound of Dave's key in the lock. He'd be home at any moment, then she could share this heaviness.

She closed her eyes as she heard the soft sound of the opening door followed by the squeak of his shoes on the foyer tiles. "Megan?"

"In here." The pillow muffled her voice, but he had no trouble finding her. When she sat up to greet him, the look on his face told her he knew. Obviously, he'd called the doctor, too.

She stood and held out her arms, and they moved together, holding each other in a soundless embrace. Closing her eyes, she pressed her hand to the back of his head.

"I'm so sorry, honey," he whispered, his breath stirring the hair by her ear. "It's all my fault."

"Shhh." Pulling back, she pressed a finger to his lips even as fresh tears threatened to erupt. She shook her head. "You can't say that."

"But I had a feeling, and I didn't want to face it."

"Hush." She lowered her forehead to his chest, not willing to watch him take the blame. This would have to be a shared problem, not his or hers, but *theirs*. If the situation were allowed to come between them, it could separate them forever.

"We have to decide," she said, taking his hands, "what we're going to do next. We can try to conceive with a doctor's help, and there's always artificial insemination. Or we could adopt."

"I don't know what we should do." Holding her hands, he sat on the edge of the bed and pulled her down next to him. "But we'll pray about it and see how we feel—"

"I can't pray any more." She gulped hard, tears slipping down her cheeks. "I've been praying for so long. I can't pray another month. I've been praying for a sign, and this is it. Now we have to decide what we're going to do."

She turned to face him. "Honey, this afternoon I asked God to make our path clear. I told Him I'd rather have no chance for a baby than only a little chance, and I'm afraid that's what we'd be facing if we went to the doctor and investigated experimental procedures. We'd be signing on for more waiting, and struggle, and lab reports, and tests. The frustration and uncertainty, not to mention the expense, might drain us."

He absorbed this news in silence, then lifted his chin. "So you want to adopt?"

She drew a deep breath. "I've been thinking about it. We both love children, and we know there are thousands of kids who need parents. We could be parents to one of them—if we can't have our own. But I think we should check out all the options. Maybe there is medical hope for us. Maybe I was wrong to pray that prayer this afternoon—maybe I was testing God. I don't know. I just know I want a baby."

Watching her husband, Megan saw a look pass across his face, a look she recognized. She'd worn the same expression half an hour ago—when she had realized she might have to surrender her dream of a biological baby and move on.

Dave's hand reached up and touched her jaw, then her hair. "I was hoping for a daughter like you," he said, his voice husky.

Megan touched his cheek, and felt his tears burn her fingertips like hot wax. "A son like you would be wonderful," she whispered, "but we'll have to see what God has planned."

And then, because she had an important guest coming for dinner, Megan pushed her sorrows down, clamped a smile over them, and went out to the kitchen to begin making dinner.

Megan toyed with a wilting lettuce leaf on her plate as Dr. Comfort—Stella, in this casual environment—laughed with Dave about the child who'd brought his pet tarantula to school and turned it loose in the kindergarten classroom. "I'll never forget Miss Pritchard's face," Dave said, leaning back in his chair. "I don't think she'll ever promote 'Pet Day' again!"

"I couldn't get over the fact that the boy couldn't understand why we reacted so strongly." Stella laughed softly. "After all, he pretty much let the spider run free in his bedroom."

Dave shook his head. "I remember that boy—Ricky Feldon. I taught him the next year, in first grade. He and his family must have been cut from a different bolt of cloth— they were all creative and bright, but they definitely marched to the beat of a different drummer."

"Remember his sister, Moonglow?" Stella's blonde brows arched mischievously. "She was three years ahead of Ricky. One day she brought a book to show and tell, then proceeded to read the poems of a love-struck seventeen-year-old."

Dave frowned. "A library book?"

"Her older sister's diary!"

Megan reflexively joined in the laughter, but her thoughts were drifting far from the current conversation. She looked at Dave—six-three, handsome, and as appealing on the inside as he was attractive. All of her girlfriends at the community college had thought him a great catch—but would any of them willingly trade places with her now? Of all the young men she had dated in high school and college, why had God led her to marry Dave? She'd been in love with several of the guys she dated, and any one of them might have made a fine husband. But God had led her to Dave Wingfield, and, as a result, he had brought her face to face with infertility.

She dropped her fork to the table and picked up her iced tea glass. Of all the physical problems Dave could have had, why did he have to have one that prevented them from having biological children? He could have been born with one leg shorter than the other . . . or without a sense of smell. He could have developed allergies, or diabetes, or epilepsy, and none of those things would have prevented him from being a father. But God had allowed Dave, a man with a unique love for children, to face a future without any kids to call his own.

She lowered her gaze as tears stung her eyes. She had to rein in her thoughts, turn them toward something useful. God had led her to Dave, and she had vowed to love him in good times and bad, in sickness and in health. And this problem wasn't his alone, it belonged to both of them. Since God had called her to this marriage—and she truly believed he had—then infertility had to be part of God's will and plan for her life as well as Dave's.

But why?

She'd lived her entire life by the rules: don't smoke, don't drink, don't have sex before marriage. Do go to church, do study hard, do get a job, do maintain a good reputation. Her name was on the dean's list at college and listed in two volumes of *Who's Who in American Universities*. She'd grown up with God, and no one could say she hadn't been at least a dutiful example of what a Christian young woman should be. She wasn't perfect, no one was, but she'd always done her best to make good choices. She'd waited for Mr. Right, and she'd been delighted to find Dave and learn that he was planning to spend his life teaching young children. He was the most giving person she had ever met, and she'd been convinced they would make a great team.

So why was God sabotaging her plans?

*The Lord knows what he is doing. He has promised to be with you in every difficulty, and he will not allow you to suffer beyond the limits of your endurance . . .*

The words echoed in her mind, a lesson learned from Sunday school classes and Bible studies of years gone by. She believed those words in her head, but that belief, springing from her rational brain, did nothing to assuage the clawing pain that ripped at her heart.

She wanted to be pregnant, she wanted a baby, she wanted to raise a baby who would be flesh of her flesh and bone of her bones. And she did not want to wait. They had been married for three years and waiting for two, and surely they had waited long enough . . .

"Honey?"

She looked up. Both Dave and Stella were staring at her.

"Stella was just saying she has to leave soon. Would you like to serve the dessert now?"

Megan felt her lips twitch in an automatic smile. "Sure. I made chocolate pie." She pushed back her chair and kept talking as she walked to the kitchen counter. "It's an old recipe, from a friend. Sometimes the cocoa doesn't dissolve, that's why you'll see these little sprinkles on top, but it should still taste okay . . ."

She stopped her mindless babbling when she heard the creak of a chair. She turned and saw Dave standing behind her, and something in his forlorn expression broke her heart.

Unable to speak, she burst into tears.


With his sobbing wife in his arms, Dave looked at his boss. "I'm sorry, Stella," he said, softening his voice. "We got a bit of bad news today. Apparently . . . . well, it looks like we're not going to have children in the usual way."

The older woman's eyes closed for a moment, then she nodded slowly. "I didn't know you were trying, but I should have guessed. After all, you've been married for a while now, and I know you both love children . . ."

Her voice trailed off as Dave pressed his hand to the back of Megan's head. He had never felt more helpless in his life.

"I'm okay," Megan said, sniffing. She lifted her head and wiped away tears. "I'm so sorry. I didn't mean to blubber in the middle of dinner."

Stella stood, then reached out and placed a hand on both Dave's and Megan's shoulders. "My friends," she said, her voice breaking with huskiness, "you two are precious people. I know God has something special in store for you. But nothing worthwhile is easy, my friends. If it were, we wouldn't appreciate it like we should."

Her eyes closed for a moment, then opened. "I'd like to share a proverb with you: 'Hope deferred makes the heart sick; but when the desire comes, it is a tree of life.'"

She smiled, her eyes shining with beautiful candor. "Not *if* the desire comes, Dave and Megan, but *when*. This is God's promise for you. Trust Him."

She gave Megan a quick hug. "The pie looks delicious, my dear, but I ought to be going. I think you and Dave need some time alone."

Dave stepped forward to see her to the door, but she waved at him over her shoulder as she picked up her purse. "Never mind me, I'll see myself out. Thank you for the dinner, Megan. Thank you both for the fellowship . . . and the trust." She gave Dave a confident smile. "I'll be praying for your future—concerning your child and your job. I know you'd make an excellent principal, Dave. I'm curious to see how the Lord will work things out."

Dave waited until he heard the click of the front door, then he turned to Megan, who stood at the kitchen counter, her woebegone gaze fastened to the speckled chocolate pie.

"I want to show you something, honey." He pulled a photograph from his wallet. "Do you remember this day?"

16

He gave her the picture and waited while she studied it. He had taken the photo nearly six years before, just after they began to date. Megan had come to see him at the school where he taught, and during a lunch break she'd spent some time reading picture books to the first-graders. One little girl, a blonde, blue-eyed waif called Daniella, had stolen Megan's heart. They'd made such a pretty pair, Daniella with her blonde hair and Megan with her brunette, that Dave had snapped a picture of Daniella sitting on Megan's lap. Later, when he explained that Daniella was a foster child, Megan's eyes had filled with tears. And at that moment, he decided to marry Megan Myers.

Her eyes were flowing again as she stared at the snapshot.

"I fell in love with you that day," he whispered, leaning against the counter, "because I knew any woman who loved kids as much as I did would be a wonderful wife and mother. Nothing has changed, Meg. You're still the same girl, and you'll still make a wonderful mother."

Her lower lip trembled, but she didn't speak.

"Daniella needed a home . . . and though I don't know what happened to her, I know there are thousands like her in foster care. We can be parents, Meg. I think we can find a child fairly quickly if we're willing to accept one as old as Daniella."

Megan bit her lip as she traced the little girl's image with her fingernail. "I'd forgotten her name," she said, her voice wavering. "But I could never forget her."

Reaching out, Dave drew his wife into the circle of his arms. "We will have a child," he promised. "You'll see."


The next afternoon, Megan said goodbye to Mrs. Leber, Princess, and the five newborn pups (two big black males, one big tan female, and two tiny black-and-white spotted females with pointy faces and oversized ears), then pulled her sack lunch and can of soda from the staff refrigerator. Dr. Duncan was holed up in his office, munching on a tuna

17

sandwich between follow-up calls, so she knew she'd have a good half hour to eat and think in relative quiet.

The veterinary hospital bordered a community park, a quiet place for lunch, particularly in the humid heat of July. With her lunch bag and a book, Megan walked down the narrow path to her favorite bench, then spread her chips and sandwich on a paper towel. She hadn't felt like preparing much this morning, so her sandwich was peanut butter and jelly—not very creative, but filling.

The afternoon air was warm and sprinkled with sunlight that dropped through the dense canopy of oaks. Chewing on her sandwich, Megan turned away from the sight of a young couple sprawled on a blanket a few yards down the path. College students, from the looks of them, a young couple in love.

Insects filled the air with a continuous omnipresent churr as she hesitated and swallowed the thick peanut butter. Did that young couple dream of marriage and babies? Probably not. These days marriage seemed trivial to most people, and most career women regularly postponed motherhood until they had established their careers.

But Megan had wanted a baby almost immediately after her marriage. Two years of community college had resulted in a degree that enabled her to work as a certified veterinary technician, a job she'd hoped to keep until she married and had children. Dave was only two months shy of thirty on their wedding day, so a honeymoon baby would have been a surprise blessing. Megan knew she and Dave were in love, committed to their marriage, and committed to God's plan for their lives. A baby would only have increased their joy.

A mosquito buzzed around her ear, and she swatted it away. How odd that some people conceived easily, and others struggled for months. In the last two years she had often read the biblical stories of Hannah, who prayed for a child so fervently that the priest thought her drunk, and Rachel, who clung to her husband and cried, "Give me children or I will die!"

In her Sunday school days she hadn't been able to understand how the lack of children could darken a woman's soul . . . but now she knew that agony all too well.

Her gaze drifted to the edge of a sandbox, where a dark-haired woman sat with a blond, blue-eyed toddler in denim overalls. A boy.

As much as she wanted to look away, she couldn't. The sight of the child intoxicated her starved senses. Who was this woman who tended him, and what had brought them to the park? The woman could not be his mother—that fair-skinned child couldn't possibly have sprung from her genes. It was always possible that the boy's father was of Nordic descent, but it was far more likely that the woman was a nanny or babysitter.

Megan crinkled her nose in speculation. After working with so many canine breeds, her thoughts routinely wandered toward questions about bloodlines and heredity. If she had a nickel for every time someone brought in a pound pup and asked, "What do you think he is?" she could have retired two years ago. She'd grown adept at looking for the dark tongue of a Chow, the pushed-in faces of Pugs and Pekes, and soft, snubbed Labrador noses . . .

She looked again at the unlikely pair near the sandbox. Could the boy be adopted?

The memory of last night's conversation with Dave pricked at her nerves. He had been eager to embrace the idea of adoption, but he was thinking of adorable children like Daniella who needed homes. And she knew he didn't care for doctors and hospitals. It had taken nearly two years for him to agree to fertility testing.

But he shouldn't be so quick . . . because he didn't understand what he'd indirectly asked Megan to give up. For a man, the experience of pregnancy and childbirth was practically a moot point. But he would never have to sit in a circle of women and remain silent as they swapped stories of back pains and labor and lactation . . . all the things that bound women together in a sorority of motherhood. He would never have to congratulate his friends on their impending arrivals when his own arms ached to protectively enclose a burgeoning belly; in a department store he would never walk the long way around in an effort to avoid the infant department.

Was she being selfish? Megan bit her lip. She didn't want to feel like a martyr, but she couldn't help it. In the past few months she had silently endured more hope and pain and agony than her friends and family would ever understand. Just last week her friend Shelia had stopped her in the church vestibule. With one hand on her own pregnant belly, Shelia had looked at Megan with sharp brown eyes and said, "No luck yet, honey? Maybe you and Dave just need to get away. You know—so you can relax."

Megan clenched her teeth at the memory. *Relax?* Shelia's comment had only wound her emotions tighter. She'd left church ready to scream, and things didn't get any easier when in the parking lot the pastor called out, "Good to see you, Dave and Megan." He then looked down at his wife, and, his voice booming, said, "Remember when we were young and not saddled with kids? Those two don't know how lucky they are!"

Megan felt about as lucky as a black cat.

The woman and baby were leaving now, piling a bucket and plastic shovel into a denim bag that overflowed with books and toys. Megan smoothed her features and took another bite of her sandwich, deliberately looking away, but a moment later she found herself staring straight into the boy's bright blue eyes.

"Excuse us for interrupting your lunch," the woman said, an apologetic smile on her face. She spoke with a slight trace of an accent, reinforcing Megan's belief that the pair could not be related. "But Andre wanted to give you something."

Surprised, Megan looked again at the boy, who wordlessly held up a dandelion between chubby little fingers.

"For me?" The words caught in Megan's throat.

The woman nodded. "He likes to give presents. And if I

don't let him give it to you, he'll fight me all the way back to the car."

Megan leaned closer and held out her hands. "I would love a flower."

The wide blue eyes blinked once, then the boy edged forward and dropped the dandelion into Megan's cupped hands.

Megan couldn't stop a smile from stealing over her face. "Thank you, Andre."

The boy beamed for an instant, then tugged on the woman's hand and pointed to the dandelion-studded field beyond, eager to repeat his performance.

The woman sighed and released him. "All right, but just one more," she called as the boy toddled away.

Megan sat silently, watching him zigzag toward another dandelion.

"He's such a handful," the woman said, crossing her arms. "But I wouldn't trade him for anything."

"Your son?" Megan asked.

"Yes." The woman's voice softened. "Thank heaven."

Megan glanced up. A hint of wetness shone in the lady's eyes.

"Forgive my curiosity," Megan said, shifting her gaze to the boy again. "But I was wondering if his father is blonde and blue-eyed."

The woman let out a laugh. "He's Nigerian."

Shock flew through Megan. "African?"

The lady laughed again. "We are an international family. I am from Spain, my husband from Nigeria, and Andre is from Romania."

"Then—" Megan sat back, amazed. "You adopted him."

The woman held her head up in the hard light of the summer sun and for the first time Megan realized that she was speaking to a woman well past prime childbearing years. "Obviously," she said, her voice soaked in politeness.

Megan bit her lip as a hundred questions bubbled to her lips. Could she ask? Or would she be prying personal information from a perfect stranger?

"My husband and I," she began, looking at her hands, "are thinking about adoption. But I'm not sure I'm ready to give up the idea of having a baby of my own."

"Your *own?*" A thread of reproach filled the woman's voice. "I hate to tell you this, dear, but no child is truly your own. Children may come from the wombs of women, but all of them spring from the hand of God. They are only placed in our safekeeping for a little while."

Megan nodded, reluctantly agreeing. "But you know what I mean—I wanted a natural child."

"Look at that boy there." The woman waited until Megan lifted her gaze. "Do you see anything *unnatural* about him?"

Again Megan felt the sting of rebuke. "That's not what I meant," she whispered, feeling as awkward as a baby taking his first tottering steps. "I wanted to be pregnant. To experience everything."

"Dear lady," the woman answered, her eyes darkening with emotion, "adoption is a life experience, just like childbirth. You'll have a time of waiting and a time of hard labor. You'll feel every pain and every joy. And when the child finally comes home, you'll call yourself blessed."

Andre came toddling forward now, his mouth spread in a gummy smile and a long-necked dandelion clenched in his fist. This flower he gave to his mother, who knelt and accepted it with a kiss, then drew him into a tight embrace.

As the woman made cooing sounds in the boy's ear, Megan lifted her head.

"May I ask what motivated you to adopt?"

The woman stopped cooing as the little boy laughed, then she released him and stood. Before leaving, she paused by Megan's bench and looked at her with eyes filled with compassion.

"Why did we adopt? Partly because of selfish reasons—my husband and I wanted a child to love. Partly because we knew there are children who need homes, and partly because we believe people ought to do more than talk about the ideals of racial reconciliation."

Her eyes softened. "But mostly because I realized that if I am faithful to teach and train, my children are the only earthly things I can take to heaven with me."

Those words remained with Megan long after the last of the dandelion fuzz blew away.


The house was dense with silence when Megan came home from work. Knowing that Dave must have stayed late to help a student, she moved into the kitchen, pulled a frozen dinner from the freezer, and put it in the microwave. After punching in the numbers, she leaned against the counter and stared at the cozy room—a space that should have been cluttered by a high chair, with baby bottles in the dish drainer and a bib hanging over the edge of the sink.

She had a choice—she could whimper and moan and mourn her losses for another week or month or year, or she could move forward with her husband. After her encounter at the park, the former option seemed petty and selfish. Andre's mother was right—life was a cafeteria of rich experiences. Her tray would simply be filled with different choices than the average woman's.

She ran her hand over the spotless counter, then caught sight of Dave's photograph. He had snapped the picture as Daniella sat on Megan's lap at the child-sized book table. Their heads were a study in contrasts, one blonde, one brunette, but the same joy lit their smiles.

After pulling a marker from the junk drawer, Megan wrote the date on the back. Then she rummaged for the tape dispenser, found it, and pulled off a piece. Carefully wrapping the tape into a sticky circle, she applied it to the back of the picture, then pressed the photograph to the refrigerator.

She was standing before the fridge when Dave came in and wrapped her in a bear hug. "Something smells good."

· "Something looks good," she answered.

"Whaddya mean? You can't see me."

23

She pulled her arm free and pointed to the refrigerator. "I'm looking at that."

She felt his arms tighten around her when he realized the significance of her words. "Does this mean . . ." he let his voice fade away.

"Let's adopt one or two just like her." Turning, Megan slid her arms around his neck. "And if that goes well, we can try for three or four. Let's take as many as we can handle."

Dave looked at her, his eyes wide and questioning, then his mouth relaxed into a surprised smile. "Let's do it," he whispered, pushing a lock of hair away from her cheek. "I'm with you, Meg."

"And I'm with you, honey, no matter what." She waited until a sudden rise of emotion died down and she could control her wavering voice. "For as long as it takes, no matter what it takes. Let's wait on the Lord and see what He has in mind for this family."

Then she stood on tiptoe and pressed her lips to her husband's, hope and promise and acceptance all mingled in her kiss.

# THREE

Two months later, on an unseasonably warm afternoon in September, Megan clung to Dave's hand as they followed a winding sidewalk to a small brick building. A painted sign hung on the wall beside the glass door: *Central Virginia Social Services.*

A confusing rush of anticipation and dread whirled inside her as Dave opened the door. She'd made this appointment only a few days after their decision to pursue adoption, and during the intervening weeks she had read every book she could find on the process. She consoled her impatient heart with the knowledge that they were moving forward, and her reading had armed her with at least a cursory knowledge of what to expect in the process known as a home study. The Alta Vista social worker, Belinda Bishop, would investigate to determine whether she and Dave would be fit parents. And if she approved them, after completing her report she would place their names into a state database of waiting parents. When a child in Virginia became available, the database would be scanned for a possible match.

The process was simple and straightforward . . . and might possibly prove to be the most dreadful experience of her life.

The plain tile floor in the social services building was worn and dull, but clean. Fluorescent lights hummed overhead and shone upon glossy beige walls in the narrow corridor. Dave paused beside a door bearing a nameplate: Belinda Bishop. The door to the office stood open, and at the sound of his hesitant rap, the woman at the desk inside lifted her head.

Without being told, Megan might have guessed this

woman was a social worker. Belinda Bishop had shoulder-length brown hair, wire-rimmed glasses, and wore a long skirt with long-sleeved, full-cut blouse. The only trace of makeup upon her smooth face was a hint of lip gloss. The eyes that shone from behind the glasses were friendly and open.

"Mr. and Mrs. Wingfield?" she asked, standing. She stepped out from behind the desk and offered her hand first to Megan, then to Dave. "I've been expecting you."

As Megan and Dave murmured brief "pleased-to-meet yous," Belinda picked up a folder, then gestured toward the hallway. "My office is really too cramped for meetings like this. There's a conference room down the hall."

They followed her to another room, still small, but unencumbered with heavy furniture. A sofa sat against the far wall, a faded wing chair faced it. A toy box sat off to the side, and above it, a bulletin board featured several black and white pictures of smiling children—all school age, Megan thought, noticing how many were missing their front teeth. First grade and up, from the looks of them.

Belinda gestured toward the sofa, and Megan and Dave sat down. Dave immediately reached for Megan's hand, and she didn't resist. Any physical display of marital harmony had to help their cause . . . or would Belinda think they were pretending in an attempt to aid their case?

"Well, now." Belinda sat in the wing chair, placed her hands together, and leaned forward in a position of earnestness. "I'm delighted you're interested in adoption. As I explained on the phone, this meeting will officially begin our home study process. I'll take six weeks to get to know you, I'll inspect your home, and we'll collect the necessary documents for your case file."

Dave's forehead creased. "What sort of paperwork is required?"

Megan felt a twinge of conscience. Knowing that Dave was preoccupied with the administrative details of a new school year, she hadn't shared everything she'd learned in her telephone conversation with Ms. Bishop. Would his question make this woman think they didn't communicate in their marriage?

The social worker smiled. "We'll need a complete financial statement from you," she said, her charm bracelet jingling as she clasped her hands. "You don't have to be wealthy to adopt, but we do have to be sure you can support a child. We'll also need a statement from your medical doctor to show that you are in good health and physically able to care for a child. We'll also ask for several letters of reference from your family and friends. We're not trying to pry, but we do try to make every effort to be sure our children are going to families who can provide healthy, stable homes."

"We understand, Ms. Bishop," Megan said.

"Please, call me Belinda." The warmth of the woman's smile echoed in her voice, and Megan felt warmed by the sound of it. "We're going to know each other well by the time this is finished, so we might as well be on a first name basis."

Dave nodded. "After the home study—what then? How long will the adoption take?"

Belinda sighed heavily, as if she'd answered the question many times before.

"I can't give you a definite answer, Dave. Once your home study is complete, you'll be waiting with many other couples in the state of Virginia. When a child is entered into the system and cleared for adoption, every couple is evaluated as to suitability. Sometimes a match is made quickly. Other couples wait longer, some for several years. It all depends upon the children's needs."

Her head lifted as she met Megan's gaze. "Please understand this—we're not here to find children for parents, though that is one happy byproduct of our work. We're here primarily to find homes for children. The kids are our first priority and concern. I'll be honest—most of our children come to us from families who either could not or would not take care of them. We don't often encounter pregnant girls who make adoption plans for their babies. Most of those young women make arrangements with private adoption agencies . . . if they carry their babies to term. With abortion these days—" She shrugged. "Well, there are fewer babies available for adoption than ever."

Dave tapped his thigh. "We understand—Megan's been reading a lot. We've investigated private adoption and international adoption, but we simply can't afford the fees. And we know about the kind of children you place. Megan has also read a lot about the adoption of an older child, and the adoption of a sibling group."

Megan winced inwardly. He said *she* was reading—would Belinda think Dave didn't care? Or that this was all Megan's idea? It wouldn't be good if the social worker thought their marriage was one-sided, or that Megan wanted the adoption more than Dave did . . .

Unruffled, Belinda smiled again. "It's good that you've thought about your options. The more open you are, the more likely we are to match you with a child. But we don't handle international adoption. Because we are a state government agency, most of our children come from Virginia. We can cooperate with other agencies, of course, but we don't have access to their children."

She paused a moment and searched their faces. "If you don't have any other questions, let me explain how the home study works. We'll meet five more times—once a week, ideally, but I never know what my schedule is going to permit. In our next meeting we'll talk about your history as a couple. The next week, I'll meet with you, Dave, and the next week I'll want to meet with Megan alone. The fifth week we'll talk about the type of child you feel capable of parenting, and the sixth and final visit will take place in your home."

She pulled a sheaf of papers from her folder and extended them to Megan. "In the mean time, I'd like you to take this application with you. You can bring it back next week or mail it in, which ever you prefer. But I'll need the names and addresses of your references as soon as possible so I can send out a letter of inquiry. The sooner we get the paperwork started, the sooner we'll be finished."

Megan accepted the papers and gave them a quick glance. The application seemed fairly straightforward, followed by medical forms, a blank financial statement, and a page requesting the names and addresses of relatives and close friends.

Her fingers burned to reach for her pen. If given ten minutes, she could have most of these pages filled out . . . but she didn't want to appear overeager. Social workers probably frowned on prospective parents with no self-control.

"Thank you, Belinda," she said, folding the pages and slipping them into her purse. "I'm sure I'll be mailing them in. They don't look too complicated."

"That's good." Belinda clasped her hands together again, charms jangling on her wrist. "Any questions before you go?"

Megan looked at Dave, who merely shrugged.

"Next week?" Megan asked, breaking the silence. "Same time, same place?"

Belinda pulled out her appointment book, pulled a pencil from behind her ear, and frowned at the page. "I'm sorry, but I have to be at a conference next week. It looks like we'll have to settle for Monday of the week after next. Let's see—that'll be September 20."

Megan steeled herself to keep from grimacing. Now that they had committed themselves to the process of adoption, she wanted to get on with it, to keep the wheels in motion. She'd already had to wait two months for this initial meeting . . . but what else could she do?

She pasted on a smile that felt false. "We'll see you on September 20, then. And I'll mail in the list of references within the next day or two."

"That'll be great."

Belinda Bishop stood. Following her cue, Megan and Dave rose, too, and followed her out, walking with her as far as her office before sending her a departing smile.

As they walked from the building to the car, Megan felt as though her face were melting. Her stiff smile drooped along with her shoulders. "Well," she said, when Dave climbed in beside her, "that was . . . interesting."

"It went fine," Dave answered, turning the key. "Don't worry, honey."

Megan bit her lip and looked out the window. Easy for him to say. He wasn't second-guessing himself at every turn.

On Friday, Megan left the veterinary hospital and drove to Roberta's, a yuppie restaurant located two blocks from E.C. Glass High School. Ten minutes after twelve, a sparkling black Mustang zipped into the parking lot.

Megan glanced again at her watch. Melanie was late, as usual. Honestly, you'd think a high school senior could manage to be on time to *something* . . .

She frowned as her sister hopped out of the car, slung her purse over her shoulder, then jogged toward the bench where Megan waited. "Hey, Sis!"

"You're late." Megan shielded her eyes from the sun as her younger sister approached. Melanie was eighteen, just beginning her senior year, and the baby of the family. Five years Megan's junior, she was lean, leggy, and lovely. The striking combination of her dark hair and bright blue eyes rarely failed to turn masculine heads. Her smile could light up a marquee.

Megan's frowned deepened as her sister drew nearer. The girl wore a tight sweater and a skirt that must have required a crowbar to enter and exit.

Breathless, Melanie dropped down onto the bench beside Megan. "I wasn't sure you'd remember."

Megan blew hair out of her eyes. "I'm not old enough to be senile."

Megan grinned. "Yeah, but you said—"

"Never mind what I said. I disagree with Senior Skip Day, but if you're going to skip school, that's your decision, not mine. And, like I said, I have to eat."

Melanie grinned and pinched Megan's arm. "Loosen up, Miss Goody-goody. And let's go in. I'm starved."

Megan reluctantly followed her sister into the restaurant. They'd held senior skip day when she was in high school, too, but only the hoodlums observed it. Now, Melanie assured her, *everyone* celebrated it, and any seniors silly enough to go to school on senior skip day found themselves in an all-day study hall. Megan finally agreed to meet Mel for lunch when her sister assured her that their mother knew and approved of her plan. So now they sat in Roberta's, pondering the menu and trying to decide between fajitas and pita bread sandwiches . . .

"Megan Myers, I haven't seen you in *ages!*"

Megan glanced up when a familiar voice broke into her concentration. Debbie Jennings, a friend from Megan's high school days, stood at the edge of the booth . . . behind a swollen, terribly-pregnant belly.

"Debbie!" Forcing a smile, Megan focused on her friend's eyes. "It's Megan Wingfield now. And how are you?"

"Fine—well, great with child, obviously." Debbie pressed her hand to the small of her back and leaned on the table. "Honestly, I can't wait for this kid to pop out. I was in labor with Bobby Junior for twenty-two hours, so I'm hoping this one will come quick."

Megan freshened her smile. "Your second?"

Debbie groaned. "Yes, and I don't know why I ever wanted to be pregnant. I haven't seen my toes in three months." She hesitated and tilted her head toward Megan. "You have kids yet?"

"Not yet." Megan looked toward the menu. "I'm working at Dr. Duncan's veterinary hospital, and my husband's an assistant principal at Valley View. We're pretty busy."

"You're lucky." Debbie shifted her weight. "Nearly everyone from our class is pregnant now—when I was in the gynecologist's office last week, I thought I'd wandered into a high school reunion! Laurie, Alma Joy, Diane, Susie, Donna, Kathy, and Gail are due in the next three months, and Ruth, Susan, Sharon, and Becky have new babies."

"Honey, I wondered where you went." Bobby Wilson,

31

whom Megan dimly remembered as a high school football player, came up behind Debbie and tenderly laid a hand on her belly. "The car's waiting at the curb."

Debbie nodded at her husband, then twiddled her fingers at Megan. "I gotta go. But have fun with the puppies and kitties, okay?"

"Sure." Megan bit her lip as the Wilsons walked away, then turned her attention back to the menu. Beyond the expanse of plastic-coated paper, Melanie began to babble about her boyfriend, Todd.

Huddled over the menu, Megan slumped into morose musings. Was the entire *world* having babies? Was everyone her age pregnant or nursing? Yet it wasn't a pregnancy she wanted—she wanted to love a child.

Debbie Wilson had two children, one born and one about to be born, and she'd had the nerve to call Megan *lucky*. What did she know? Women like her got pregnant without half trying. She'd probably have a baby every year and then gripe about stretch marks and the burdens of motherhood.

Megan would give anything for just one of those burdens. She'd gladly surrender her job, her time, her energy, even her identity, just for the honor of being called Mom.

"You're not listening, Megan!"

Blinking, Megan lifted her head. Across the table, Melanie's eyes were wide and her lips pursed in a petulant frown.

"I'm sorry. Were you talking to me?"

Melanie's blue eyes flashed. "And who else is in this booth? You haven't heard a word I've said, have you?"

Megan dropped her menu. "Sorry. I've had a few things on my mind."

"I was telling you about Todd. Mom and Dad don't like him."

Megan inhaled a deep breath, bracing herself for the inevitable. "So—why do you keep going out with him?"

Megan flipped her hair over her shoulder. "I dunno. Because he likes me. Because he makes me feel special. It's, like, all the other guys are so immature, but Todd's really cool."

As Melanie rattled on, Megan propped her elbow on the table and rested her chin in her hand. Time to play big sister. But it was okay—Melanie certainly wouldn't understand what Megan and Dave were going through.

"Tell me all about it," she said, smiling.


On a cold, windy October night, Megan lowered her head into her fur collar and followed Dave into the social services building. Belinda had suggested that they attend at least one meeting of an adoptive parents' support group, and, in an effort to prove how eager they were to Do Things Properly, she and Dave had made plans to attend the first meeting after the commencement of their home study.

There were already a dozen people in the conference room when they entered, and by the way they were laughing around the coffee maker, Megan guessed they knew each other pretty well. Their children, apparently, were in the care of babysitters or friends, for there were no children in the room.

Belinda greeted them with a smile, then glanced at her watch and clapped her hands for attention. "Welcome people," she called, her voice cutting through the congenial chatter. "I'd like to introduce our newcomers—Dave and Megan Wingfield, prospective adoptive parents. They are currently involved in the home study process."

Megan felt herself blushing as a dozen pairs of eyes turned in their direction. A few brows lifted, but most faces wore understanding smiles.

Belinda moved to the folding chairs. "If you'll all find a seat, we can begin. Tom, I think you are the moderator of this meeting. Why don't you get us started?"

Megan slipped out of her coat and took a seat next to Dave while the others left the coffee maker and made their way to seats in the circle. Glancing around, Megan tried to find a common denominator that marked these people, but she could see nothing obvious. The men and women in the room represented every race and age. If clothing could be trusted as a guide, they also represented several different income levels.

Tom, a balding, middle-aged man in Gucci loafers, stood and rubbed his hands together. "All right. Who has an issue they'd like to bring before us?"

A heavy woman in a plaid sweater lifted her hand. "Something happened to me this week. My little Michael—" she paused as the others nodded, for apparently she'd discussed him before, "threw a temper tantrum in the grocery store this week. He was crying because I wouldn't buy him a bag of candy, but my mother-in-law, who has never really approved of our adoption, declared that he was crying because he missed his *real* mother!"

The woman slapped her hands upon her blue-jeaned thighs. "Now how am I supposed to handle *that*? I wanted to slug her."

Megan sat, stunned and silent, while the other parents made suggestions. Then another couple announced that they and their child had just moved from the *honeymoon* to the *protest* stage.

"There are stages?" Dave whispered in her ear.

"I guess so," she whispered back.

Tom, the moderator, scratched his chin as the conversation died down. "I think the thing that bothers me the most is the vocabulary people use with regard to adoption," he said. "People speak of birth mothers as *real* mothers or *natural* mothers, but adoptive mothers and fathers are the real psychological parents. And we speak of birth mothers who *give up* their babies, as if that's either really noble or pathetic. It's so much more accurate to say they *make an adoption plan* for their children."

"The one I can't stand," another woman inserted, "is when people meet my twins and then ask if I have kids *of my own*. As if these two don't belong to me!"

An African-American mother waved her hand. "You think

that's bad? I have two, you know—LaShonda and Kareem—and the other day someone asked me if they were brother and sister. I said, 'They are now!'"

Belinda Bishop giggled. "I can top that. I have a friend who's recently adopted an infant from Korea. She was at the pediatrician's office the other day with her three-month-old, when a woman asked if the child spoke English! As if the baby could speak anything!"

As the group erupted in laughter, Megan caught Dave's eye. Like the rest of the world, she and Dave and undoubtedly been violating adoption taboos for years, as ignorant as anyone who had never explored the delicate art of grafting a branch onto a family tree.

She reached out and squeezed his hand. They had a lot to learn, but they were willing. And ready.

On the third Monday in November, over two months after beginning their home study, Megan stood in the middle of her small living room and regarded the area with a critical eye. The floors were freshly vacuumed, the sofa pillows plumped, and she'd spent most of Saturday washing and ironing the full muslin curtains. The room—the entire house, in fact—was as spotless as she could make it. Dave had tiptoed out this morning, afraid he'd make tracks in the rug or spill water droplets on her gleaming kitchen counters.

In less than a quarter-hour, Belinda Bishop was to come for their final meeting, the home visit. She had assured Megan and Dave that this would be an informal time, more of a cursory check than a white-glove inspection. The home visit was only required to be certain that the department of social services wasn't placing a child into a dangerous environment.

Despite Belinda's assurances, Megan had baked chewy chocolate chip cookies and prepared a pitcher of sweet tea a Southern favorite. The pitcher and platter of cookies now sat on the kitchen table, a pretty spread that might appeal to Belinda's mid-afternoon appetite. Whether or not the social worker succumbed to the culinary treats, Megan couldn't imagine a less dangerous environment for a child. Throughout the house, she'd pulled up all the electrical cords, put rubber stoppers in the outlets, and screwed childproof locks into all the cabinets.

She wiped the kitchen counter again, then folded the dish towel and hung it on the rod hidden tucked beneath the sink. Then she moved through the house one last time, checking the bathroom, the master bedroom, and finally, the small bedroom meant for their child.

She'd begun to decorate it the week after they began their home study. Belinda's patient confidence and unflagging support encouraged Megan enough that she felt confident to buy paint and wallpaper, and each weekend she'd worked on one particular aspect of the room she intended to be their nursery. Dave had installed a chair rail, then Megan painted it with white enamel to match the tall dresser from her mother's house. Dazzling yellow paint covered the walls from the chair rail to the ceiling, and a bright rainbow wallpaper in primary colors decorated the space between the railing and the soft green carpeting.

The room looked large, bright, and empty. They hadn't bought a bed, not knowing the age of the child they would welcome home, and they'd chosen primary colors because they didn't know if they'd be getting a boy or a girl. Or both.

Megan leaned against the wall as her thoughts drifted back to last week's meeting with Belinda. At the outset she had warned them that she would ask difficult questions, and she'd been right. To her surprise, Megan had discovered that her willingness to parent had unexpected limits.

"Would you consider a child of rape?" she'd asked. Megan and Dave both nodded eagerly.

"Would you consider a sibling group?"

"The more the merrier," Dave answered, grinning. "I'm with kids all day, so more than one is no problem."

Belinda made a note on her pad and moved on. "Would you consider a child who is biracial or of another race? We try to discourage interracial adoption because we feel children should grow up with parents from the same background and culture. But sometimes it is in the child's best interest to make an exception."

Megan thought of Andre and his mother. "No problem," she said.

"In some communities, a mixed family will encounter difficulties," Belinda said, a warning note in her voice. "You have to think about this."

"We'd never live any place our children wouldn't be welcome," Dave answered. Megan shot him a look of gratitude.

"Would you consider," Belinda consulted her list, "a child whose biological parent suffered from schizophrenia?"

Megan made a face. "I don't know much about mental illness. Are such things hereditary?"

Belinda tilted her head. "The evidence is not conclusive, but it suggests they can be."

Megan closed her eyes. Nothing in her lifetime had prepared her for dealing with mental illness—no one in her family had ever suffered from it. She felt certain God would give her grace and strength for anything that came her way, but would she be foolish to volunteer for a struggle He might not have intended to give her? Would answering negatively jeopardize their chances for receiving a child?

"I've had no experience with schizophrenia," she said slowly, looking at Dave. "I think we could handle anything that came our way after the child became part of our family—"

Dave picked up her thought. "But perhaps we shouldn't go on record as approving that choice," he said, his voice firm. "A mental illness like bipolar disorder would be difficult for us."

Belinda inclined her head in a matter-of-fact gesture. "Would you consider a child with a learning disability?"

"Yes," Dave answered without hesitation.

"Would you consider a child who needed elective surgery

such as the correction of a cleft palate?"

Megan nodded. "Yes. We have good health insurance."

"Would you consider a child who needed braces? Orthodontia is not usually covered by health insurance."

Megan closed her eyes. She'd never dreamed she'd have to consider so many options. This experience was almost like choosing between options in a new car—but this was a *child*, not a clump of steel and fiberglass.

"Braces aren't a problem," Dave answered. "Somehow, we'll make it work."

"Now let's talk about age," Belinda said, adjusting her tone as she pulled out another sheet of paper. "You've stated your preference for an infant. Would you consider a child up to two years old?"

Megan smiled. "Yes."

"Up to three?"

"Of course. We've discussed it, and we'd be happy to accept any child of preschool age."

Belinda had glanced at her notes again. "Okay, what about a sibling group—one infant, one child school age?"

The sound of the front door's click snapped Megan out of her reverie. She glanced at her watch. Dave was ten minutes late, but she'd forgive him if he remembered to bring the fresh-cut flowers for the kitchen table.

She found him in the foyer, bouquet in hand.

"Thanks," she said, taking the bundle from his hand. "Let me put these in water. Did you have trouble getting away from school?"

"No, Dr. Comfort covered for me." He followed her into the kitchen. "And I brought home some work to do this evening . . . afterward."

Megan filled the vase with water, then snipped the stems from the long-stemmed daisies and placed them in the water. She barely had time to pull them into a pleasing shape before the doorbell rang.

# FOUR

Dave followed the women, his hands in his pockets and his thoughts wandering as he toured his own house. Despite Megan's casual demeanor, he could tell she felt nervous. She laughed more frequently than usual, and her voice sounded tight and strained.

Belinda, on the other hand, seemed as unflappable as always. She simply walked through the house and smiled as Megan pointed out the bathrooms, the two bedrooms, and the new wallpaper in the nursery.

He knew Megan would spend most of her time in the bright yellow room, so when they reached it, Dave leaned against the wall, crossed his arms in a posture of polite interest, and allowed his thoughts to roam. These days Meg thought of little but the adoption and the coming child, but his job forced him to think of other things. Now that Dr. Comfort had announced her impending retirement, he had hoped that the school board would notice that he'd been given more than an assistant principal's fair share of administrative duties. Dr. Comfort had purposefully arranged to gradually shift the mantle of responsibility from her shoulders to his, but so far the school board seemed unaware of her friendly maneuvering.

"Dave and I liked this rainbow wallpaper," Meg was saying, playing Vanna White as she lifted her arms and gracefully gestured to the bright walls. "I read somewhere that primary colors are more stimulating for babies than pastels—and for small children, too, of course."

Dave repressed a sigh. Meg was at it again, second-guessing every word that slipped from her lips in Belinda's presence. She'd added the bit about small children just so Belinda wouldn't think their hearts were set upon an infant. Truthfully, they preferred a baby, but so did almost every other waiting adoptive couple. Healthy white infants were hard to find, especially if you couldn't afford to pay for a private adoption arranged by people with connections.

He didn't move in the circles of doctors and lawyers—his circle included teachers and administrators and educational bureaucrats, and lately that circle had done little but frustrate him. Instead of noticing how so many students had *improved* over the course of the Comfort/Wingfield administration, the school board had focused on a recent series of standardized exams and whipped itself into a frenzy. Because the exams indicated that Valley View students were statistically average—*only* average—they'd commissioned a demographic study of the city and unearthed a series of comparable student test scores. They bemoaned the fact that Valley View students did not test as well as a similar group in 1985, and ignored the fact that mindless television, video games, and absentee parents had undoubtedly taken their toll over the years . . .

A month ago, he'd been confident he would be the next principal of Valley View Elementary. But if the school board's demographic study revealed a population shift to the outlying suburbs, Valley View might not even *exist* next year.

He needed to discuss these things with Megan. She had a real gift for helping him to calm down, put his emotions in order, and take the long view of things. But in the last few weeks she had thought of little but Belinda's home study, and tonight she'd be too tired to do more than whisper goodnight, crawl into bed, and sleep. She had exhausted herself with concerns about the adoption, and he didn't want to burden her with yet another uncertainty.

But she had to know. Like it or not, their future was anchored to the fate of Valley View Elementary School.

Standing on the concrete front porch, Megan waved a final cheery farewell to Belinda, then stepped back into the cool shade of the foyer. As Dave turned toward the kitchen, she closed the door and leaned against it, sighing in relief.

They were finished. Done with meetings, soul-searching questions, family histories, investigations, examinations, and confessions. Belinda now knew them better than anyone outside their families, and she'd peered into practically every corner of their house. Now all the social worker had to do was collect their letters of reference, write her report, and submit it to the state. If she was any kind of a friend, she'd do those things as quickly as she could.

Megan pulled herself off the door and moved toward the kitchen, where Dave was rummaging in the refrigerator. Poor man. In all the excitement, she hadn't even *thought* about dinner.

"Hey," she whispered, coming up behind him and slipping her arms about his waist, "you want to go out for a bite? Celebrate the end of the inquisition?"

Hunched inside the open door, he froze. "I'm afraid I don't really feel much like celebrating."

His flat tone caught her by surprise. She stepped to the side and peered at his face. "You sick or something?"

His skin color was normal, his eyes set and serious. "Things at school are in a bit of an upheaval."

Relieved, she waved the matter away. "Things at school will settle down, they always do." Suddenly thirsty, she moved to the cupboard and took out a glass. "That went well, don't you think? Belinda seemed to like the house."

Dave pulled a package of bologna from the fridge. "What's not to like?"

A little annoyed by his curt tone, Megan turned and studied him. Had the home study process taken a toll on him, too? She'd tried to relieve his stress by handling all the appointments and correspondence herself, but perhaps she'd underestimated the mental burden he carried.

A malicious little voice cackled from some obscure corner

of her brain. *What* mental burden did he carry? Though she knew he wanted a child as much as she did, he'd come through the adoption process relatively unscathed. He had not had to endure the trial of knowing all his friends were pregnant. He hadn't spent more than twenty months playing pregnancy guessing games with his body and refusing to take medicine for a head cold on the chance that he *might* be pregnant. He had a job, an important career, to distract him from the waiting and the frustration, while puppies and kittens and birth and life surrounded her even at the office . . .

"Listen." Against her will, her voice trembled. "I think we've come through this pretty well, and it'd be nice if you could celebrate with me. I know things aren't always perfect at school, Dave, but school is only a job, and what we've been dealing with here is our entire *life*. Our family, our dreams for the future, who we are—all those things are wrapped up in this adoption. So I'd appreciate it if you could put the school out of your mind for a couple of hours and think about what's really important."

He turned to her, concern and confusion mixing in his eyes. "Meg, I've been with you every step of the way."

She lifted a hand. "Not quite. On the surface, sure, you've been great. But you don't know what I've been going through, Dave, not really. I haven't told you a lot of things because I didn't want to hurt you."

A sudden spasm of grief knit his brows. "You mean . . . because this is all my fault."

Wincing, Megan clutched the edge of the counter, drowning in waves of guilt. She'd promised never to bring this issue up. She had never wanted to shake her finger in his face or point to the reason why they couldn't have biological children . . . but maybe she'd been pointing all along, and had been too engrossed to realize it.

"Honey," she closed her eyes, "I love you, and I know God put us together. I don't blame you for anything, and I know God has allowed this for a reason. It's the reason I can't understand. Of all the men I know, you're the one who would make the best father, and I've wanted to be a mother since I was old enough to dress my cat in baby clothes. I've been ready, I've been willing, and I haven't been able to understand why we weren't allowed to have kids like everybody else."

She turned from him and stared at the calendar hanging over the phone. "Remember last week when I went to Susan Michael's baby shower?"

His voice came out hoarse, as if forced through a tight throat. "I was surprised you went."

"I almost didn't, but I couldn't figure out how to get out of it, with Susan having been my maid of honor and all. And I did pretty good through most of it—I sat and smiled while everybody ooed and ahhed over the gifts, and I played those silly shower games even though I felt like an automaton. But then Susan's mother came over and squeezed my shoulder, and I knew she knew what I was feeling—and something inside me snapped. I ran into the bathroom and stayed there the rest of the night. My eyes were so red from crying that I had to wait until everyone else left the party before I could even come out."

His voice faded to a whisper. "I'm sorry."

"It's not your fault." She lifted her gaze to the ceiling. "It anything, it's my fault. I'm just so tired. Tired of fighting a vicious battle against my own stubborn will and longings. Tired of trying to pretend I'm not hurting, tired of striving to be happy for other couples, tired of fighting to be patient and not explode in frustration, tired of struggling to speak of anything but the number one thought on my mind. I'm working to keep my faith, struggling to believe in God, fighting to live each day instead of willingly casting every day aside for just one tomorrow . . ."

She blinked when she felt a tear roll down her cheek. She wasn't crying, really, the tear resulted from overflowing emotion.

"I feel so alone, Dave. You are the only one who knows

what I'm going through, and yet I don't know if you can know how it feels to be a woman and not a mother."

She bowed her head as Dave's arms slipped around her shoulders. "To fight aloud is very brave," he said, in the hushed voice he often used when he whispered love poems into her ear. "But gallanter, I know, who charge within the bosom the Calvary of Woe."

She lifted her gaze to meet his. "Walt Whitman?"

"Emily Dickinson." His hand cupped against her cheek and held it gently. "You are the most gallant woman I know, Meg. And I know God is using this to prepare both of us . . . for something that lies ahead."

Megan groaned. "That's not a very comforting thought."

He laughed softly. "Then consider this—you don't have to fight any more, honey. The hard work is done. Now we wait."

Megan laughed weakly. Dave, apparently, had no idea how tough waiting could be.


Dave watched as Megan swiped at her eyes and murmured something about needing to use the bathroom. She left the kitchen, leaving him in stunned silence.

In the three years of their marriage, he had never heard such an outpouring of raw emotion. Megan was usually calm and in control, confident in her faith and steady as a rock.

He had no idea she'd been weeping in bathrooms and doubting God.

He sat down at the table and pressed his hands to his right temple, trying to massage away the pain that threatened there. He loved the idea of a baby, he wanted children, but he loved Megan more than any person on earth. Would this as yet intangible and uncertain child drive them apart?

Pressing his face into his hands, he prayed for wisdom.

# FIVE

Thanksgiving and Christmas came and went. Optimistically predicting that this would be their last Christmas without a baby, Megan and Dave spent the holiday at the Peaks of Otter Lodge, a rustic retreat atop a mountain near Roanoke.

January brought snow, February, wind. March came in like the proverbial lion and went out like a lamb, leaving the Virginia mountains covered with the green-gold sheen of Spring.

On a Saturday morning in April, Megan stubbed her toe as she hurried to catch the phone in the kitchen. "Helloooo," she moaned, massaging the injured digit as she settled the phone against her shoulder.

"Meg?" Her mother's voice seemed flatter than usual.

Megan's internal antennae snapped to attention. "What's wrong, Mom?"

She was hoping for a quick reassurance, but her mother sighed. "Have you spoken to Melanie lately?"

"Not in a while. Why?"

"She's pregnant."

Forgetting her throbbing toe, Megan slid down the wall and sat on the floor. "You're kidding."

"I wish I was. She told us last night, and she's already made her plans. She and Todd want to get married next month. The baby's due in November."

Megan's senses skittered in stunned disbelief. "She can't be pregnant, she's not the kind of girl who sleeps around. The last time I talked to her she said she and Todd were doing great, that he was a really nice guy—"

Realizing that she was babbling to cover her confusion, Megan snapped her mouth shut.

Her mother sighed audibly. "All kinds of girls get pregnant, Meg, and Todd does seem to be a nice guy. Your father and I were upset, of course, but we're beginning to think marriage is the best answer for them. That way the baby will have a home and a father—"

Megan's heart pumped outrage through her veins. "The baby will have a couple of *children* for parents! Melanie and Todd aren't ready to have a baby—why, they couldn't have survived the first *week* of our home study. They don't know each other, they have no financial security, and they don't know the first *thing* about raising a child!"

"All parents learn by trial and error, Meg."

"You sound like you're on their side!"

"Megan," her mother's voice flattened like chilled steel, "I'm on everybody's side. I want what's best for this baby, for Melanie, for Todd, and for you, honey. I know what you must be feeling."

Megan stiffened. "You could not possibly understand."

There was a short silence. "Maybe I can't," her mother finally answered, "but Melanie's situation has nothing to do with you, Meg. I only called because, well, you're her sister, and I thought you should know."

Megan bit her lip as desperation fortified her courage. "Maybe—if they really want what's best for the baby, they could give it to me and Dave. Maybe this has been the Lord's plan all along. We could adopt him, and he'd have two stable parents, but Melanie and Todd would know the baby was growing up in a good home, and Melanie could see him whenever she wanted—"

"Melanie wants this child, Meg. Somehow, believe it or not, this experience has been good for her. For the first time in months she's been focused on something other than herself. She's already been to the doctor, she's been taking her prenatal vitamins, she made sure everything was fine before she even told us the news."

Through her own regret, Megan heard the pain in her mother's voice. She drew a deep breath, realizing that the grief she felt had to be but a shadow of the anguish that had engulfed her parents. They had raised their daughters in a Christian home, they had taught their girls how to behave as examples of godly purity. One of those daughters had made a mistake.

Megan had made mistakes, too—but none so public.

She brought her hand to her forehead. "I'm sorry, Mom, about what I said before. I know this can't be easy for you or Dad. And I understand, I really do. If Melanie can love and raise this baby, then she should. It's just that—"

"You don't have to explain, Meg." Her mother hesitated a moment more, silence rolling over the telephone line, then added, "We'd appreciate your prayers. We're all going to need them."

"Okay, Mom." Megan blinked back tears and replaced the phone in its cradle.

# SIX

In May, Melanie and Todd married in a quiet ceremony in the church chapel. Megan and Dave attended the wedding, then hosted a small reception in their home. The occasion marked the first time Megan met Todd, and she later told Dave that her new brother-in-law seemed little more than a pimply-faced adolescent. He certainly didn't look like father material . . . but she couldn't and wouldn't question their decision.

Melanie was in love—with Todd, her unborn baby, and the world. The newlyweds would live with Megan's parents until the baby came and Todd graduated from high school. Then he'd find a job and go to vocational school, and Melanie would go back to her job at the local grocery store. She had promised to get her GED and think about college. Together, Megan admitted, with help, they might make their marriage work.

The next two months passed with agonizing slowness. At work, Megan went about her duties as usual. In quiet lulls she stared at the big clock above the reception desk, noticing that the minute hand seemed to struggle to move from one black notch on the dial's perimeter to the next.

Belinda had urged her to call at least once a week. "Obviously, I won't have news, or I would certainly call you," she explained at the conclusion of their home study. "But I know how hard the waiting can be, and I love to hear from my prospective parents. So call me whenever you like, just to keep in touch."

Megan rationed herself to one call per week. She marked her calendar with "Call Belinda" every Monday, and made the

48

ritual contact during her lunch break. On Monday mornings, the work seemed to go even slower than usual, the moment when she could call Belinda fluttering ahead of her like the tail of a kite. And each week, though Belinda had no concrete news to offer, that simple contact assured Megan that Belinda was alive and well, their names were percolating in the system, and the Virginia State Social Services computer was humming with good intentions to place waiting children with eager parents.

Spring melted into summer, and Megan struggled to look for the silver lining in the overhanging clouds. She and Dave took a few weekend trips to their favorite little hotels, romantic getaways that would be impossible once they had a baby to care for. They ate once a week in the town's nicest steakhouse, knowing such extravagances would be unwise once their family expanded. They stayed up late on Friday nights, slept late on Saturdays, and exploited the freedoms of childlessness. For soon, Megan told herself, this season would end.

Every day felt like a battle. Every hour was another yard gained on the field of conquest, every week a mile, every month a major victory. Months passed would never have to be relived again. Every day of waiting was one less she'd have to endure . . . if God was faithful and kept His promises.

In June, Belinda reported that she had placed one child and was working on another placement. Megan hung up the phone and breathed a sigh of relief. Maybe this activity signaled some sort of adoption baby boom, and they'd be called next.

In July, Megan was checking her makeup in the lady's room at church when a pregnant friend came in to wash her hands. "We felt the baby kick yesterday," she said, catching Megan's eye in the mirror. "Michael ran over to get the video camera, and we could actually see the little guy kicking."

Megan nodded. "That's nice."

The woman's gaze dropped to Megan's flat stomach, then her mouth wobbled in a poor imitation of a smile.

"So—have you adopted that baby yet?"

As if babies grew on trees! Megan bit back a caustic answer and shook her head. "No," she said, forcing a smile. "It takes a long time. We've been waiting nearly a year, and we might have to wait many months more."

The friend lifted her brow in surprise. "Really? Gosh, with all the people who don't want babies and abuse them, you'd think it'd be easy to get one."

The corner of Megan's mouth twisted. "It's not." Excusing herself, she left the ladies' room.

On July 13, Megan marked the one year anniversary of their "we will have no babies day" with a glass of orange juice in her kitchen. She sat alone at the breakfast table, the newspaper at her left hand, a breakfast pastry at her right.

Another year of waiting lay beyond the horizon, and she steeled herself to face it. She had recently read a quote from Samuel Johnson. He called sorrow "a kind of rust of the soul," that could be "remedied by exercise and motion."

She knew exactly what he meant. The home study experience had been difficult, but she'd found pleasure in it, for she was doing something to bring her child home. Now she could do nothing but wait, and inactivity chafed at her rusty, sorrowful soul . . . as did guilt. She was a Christian, she was supposed to have joy and faith, but both seemed as elusive as quicksilver.

What did God want of her? Did he want her to quit her job to demonstrate faith that she'd soon be a mother? She'd quit in a minute, but it seemed foolish to sit home doing nothing when she could be earning money they'd need when they became a one-income family. And God was not the author of foolishness.

Sighing, she picked up her newspaper and shook it open. Nothing to do but wait.

# SEVEN

The high-pitched warble of the bedside telephone shattered the predawn stillness. Megan sat up, as awake as if she'd been slapped from sleep by an invisible hand. She peered at the digital clock and read the glowing numerals: 5:45.

No one ever called with good news at this hour.

The room shifted dizzily as she reached for the phone. "Hello?"

She had expected to hear her mother's voice, instead a man spoke her name over a weak connection.

"Yes," she said, strengthening her voice. "This is Megan Wingfield." Beside her, Dave stirred, then lifted his head.

"Megan, this is Joe Hogan."

Megan pushed a hank of hair out of her face and struggled to place the name. She had known a Joe Hogan in high school—they'd attended the same church, then he'd gone off to college and seminary. The last bit of news about Joe Hogan had him going overseas to be a missionary somewhere . . .

"Joe Hogan—from my church?" She tried to keep the disbelief from her voice.

Joe laughed. "Bet you didn't think you've be hearing from me in the middle of the night, did you?"

Dave tugged on her arm. "Who's Joe?"

She gestured toward the lamp, feeling that somehow things might make sense if she weren't having this conversation in the dark. Light flooded the room as she asked, "Joe, why are you calling me?"

He laughed again. "This may sound crazy, Megan, but I'll

come right to the point. You probably know my wife and I are missionaries in South Korea—"

She hadn't known, but she let him continue.

"—and yesterday someone left a baby on our doorstep. This happens fairly often, you know, but it's never happened to us. Some of the nationals here think all Americans are rich, therefore, life with a rich American has to be good. Anyway, Susan and I were praying about it, and your name popped into my head. I'm pretty sure the Lord put it there."

"You thought of me? For a baby?"

Megan stared at Dave. She needed a minute to orient herself—no, she needed an *hour*. This was too sudden, too unreal. There was no earthly reason why Joe Hogan, a man she hadn't spoken to or thought of in years, should wake her in the middle of the night with news of a baby.

Why her? Why now? And why that baby?

"Joe," confusion clotted her voice, "I'm not sure what you want me to do."

The line hissed with silence, then, "Don't you know?"

Megan hesitated, blinking with bafflement. What was she supposed to do? She and Dave had investigated international adoption, but the expense had been prohibitive. They couldn't afford to pursue international adoption last year, and they certainly couldn't afford it now.

"Don't you want a baby?" Joe's voice filled her ear, insistent and strong. "I'm sure you're the one I was supposed to call."

"Yes." She whispered the word. "Yes, but things are so complicated. We're already on a waiting list here in Alta Vista."

"I don't know about you," Joe went on, as cheerfully as if he were discussing the weather, "but I'm going to see what I have to do from this end to have this little girl declared adoptable. You do what you have to from your end—and don't worry about a thing in the mean time. Susan and I will take care of her until things work out. We think she's about three months old, and she's a real sweetheart."

Megan nodded numbly into the phone. "Okay, Joe. We'll be in touch."

"What was that all about?" Dave asked as she hung up.

Megan gave him a bewildered smile. "Joe Hogan, a guy I went to church with years ago, is a missionary in Korea. He and his wife found a three-month-old on their doorstep. They seem to think we are supposed to adopt her."

Dave snorted softly as he lay back down and punched his pillow. "Was our name pinned onto the kid's diaper or something?"

"Something like that," Megan answered softly, reaching over him to switch off the lamp.

She returned to her pillow, but her whirling thoughts wouldn't let her sleep. Someone must have written the Hogans and mentioned that she and Dave were waiting to adopt. It was no secret—Megan had encouraged her friends to share the news, because you never knew when someone might hear of a frightened pregnant girl who could not mother a child. Obviously, the Hogans had heard the story, so when they found this baby they naturally thought of her and Dave.

But she'd had her hopes dashed too many times to pin them on a baby half a world away. A few weeks before, a pregnant girl who called herself Jillian had wandered into a local maternity home and applied for free care. While church members scurried to find her a place to live and a job with which she could support herself, the girl made all sorts of references to kind of family she wanted to adopt her baby. She wanted Christian parents for her child, a couple who had been married at least three years, a family who loved animals and would let the child have a dog . . .

A friend called Megan, of course, and she'd let her hopes rise, even arranging to take Jillian to lunch for a friendly let's-get-to-know-each-other meeting. Two hours before the lunch, however, one of the girls from the church office called with devastating news. There would be no baby. Jillian's pregnancy was nothing more than a sweater tucked under her dress. They might never have known if one of the other ladies hadn't seen a cardigan fall onto the floor when Jillian entered a bathroom stall . . . and realized that Jillian hadn't been wearing a sweater in the summer heat.

Megan turned onto her side, pillowing her cheek on her hand. "Why now, God?" she whispered. "If this is from you, why today and not yesterday? Why is the baby in Korea and not Virginia? And why would you lead us away from a low-cost adoption to an expensive situation we can't possibly afford?"

She listened with her heart as well as her ears, but heard no answers in the soft gray twilight.

Belinda had no answers, either. "I mentioned before that we don't do international adoptions," she said when Megan called from work. "But I'm pretty sure you can use the home study we've prepared. In most international adoptions, you work with two agencies—one in the child's country of origin and one licensed in the United States. You'll have to find out which area agency works with Korea, and you'll have to be sure the child is registered with a Korean agency who will work with the American agency. I can offer the home study I've written—which might save you time and money—and they may allow me to do the follow-up visits. But I can't handle any of the actual arrangements for this Korean child. It's not my jurisdiction."

More confused than ever, Megan hung up, then called her mother, who responded to the story with more enthusiasm than Megan felt. "God is working," her mother said, her voice filled with hope and a note of awe. "I knew He would. And He will take care of everything until that little baby is home with you."

"I'm just not sure, Mom." Megan stared at the veterinary office clock as she wrapped the phone cord around her wrist. "How do I know this is from the Lord? It could all fall apart tomorrow—"

"Ask Joe to send you pictures," her mother interrupted. "And start thinking of a name. This is a *real* little girl, Meg, and she's waiting. Stop looking at the obstacles, and think of the child. She's alive. She's in Joe's house. And she needs a home."

Buoyed by her mother's confidence, Megan disconnected the call. A thrill shivered through her senses. Could this be the child they'd been waiting for?

Ignoring Laurie's curious glance, Megan picked up the phone book, then scribbled down the number for the church office. After speaking to the receptionist, she was transferred to the missions pastor, who gave her the Hogans' phone number in Korea.

"You should probably wait until early evening to call," the pastor reminded her. "The time difference, you know."

She laughed. "I know. And thanks."

The day dragged by with remarkable slowness. At four o'clock, Megan grabbed her purse and ran out the door. At five, with Dave sitting beside her, she placed the long distance call to Korea.

"Susan?" she asked when a woman answered. "This is Megan Wingfield."

"Megan!" Susan's voice was warm and compassionate. "I've been thinking about you." In the background, Megan could hear the sound of children laughing. Not *the* baby— she'd be too young. Susan and Joe must have other children.

"We're going to do whatever we must to make this adoption work," Megan said, smiling at Dave. "And we appreciate you taking care of the baby while we wait."

"We'll do whatever we can," Susan answered, a smile in her voice. "My boys love her. She's a little angel."

The sound of a baby's gurgle echoed over the phone line, and Megan's heart clenched at the sound of it. "Is that—"

"Yes," Susan answered softly. "She's right here, on my shoulder."

Megan thought she might burst from the sudden swell of happiness that rose in her chest. "Will you," she pushed the words out, "will you call her Danielle Li? And will you send pictures? I'll reimburse you for the postage and film—"

"There's no need for that," Susan interrupted. "Just do whatever you have to, and we'll do the same on this end. I have a feeling she'll be home very soon."

"Thank you." A hot, exultant tear trickled down Megan's cheek. "You'll never know what you've done for us."


Four days later, after a series of frantic calls, Megan and Dave sat in the lounge of the Washington, D.C. office of Welcome Home, an international adoption agency with official ties to South Korea. Though the office was nearly a five hour drive from their house, the agency served Virginia, Maryland, and the District of Columbia.

Megan clutched the folder on her lap—it contained a letter from Belinda Bishop, a sealed copy of their home study report, their birth certificates, and a copy of their marriage license. In her purse, safely tucked away, she carried an application for a second mortgage on their home—a logical, practical answer to their financial dilemma. As soon as they knew how much the adoption would cost, they planned to apply for a loan.

Megan felt edgy after the four-hour drive from Alta Vista. The last thing she wanted to do was sit in a waiting room, but from this point every day counted. She was no longer waiting on a nebulous, chimerical child—she was working for a little girl living temporarily with the Hogans in Seoul, South Korea.

Megan ached to work the rust off her soul.

The door to the inner office finally opened. A tall, slender woman stepped out and shook their hands, introducing herself as Helen Gresham, a senior social worker for Welcome Home.

Megan nearly collapsed in relief at the sight of Helen's gentle demeanor and sparkling blue eyes. She hadn't realized how nervous she was until she sat before Helen's desk and the tension went out of her shoulders.

"I understand that you've done quite a bit of the work for us," Helen said, lowering herself into the worn leather chair behind her cluttered desk. "This is an unusual situation, but everything seems in order. I don't really foresee any problems, but I have to ask you a few questions." She smiled as she caught Megan's gaze. "You understand."

Megan nodded. "Of course." She felt as though she had been answering questions for the last year. She no longer had a private life, secrets, or untold confessions. She'd relay any detail of her past life if doing so would bring finally their baby home.

She reached for Dave's hand and held it as they again answered questions about their families, their backgrounds, and their marriage. During the session, the door to Helen's door opened and an Asian woman entered, dropped a pile of mail on the social worker's desk, and slipped away.

Helen looked up and paused a moment to riffle through the mail. Her smile broadened as she picked up an envelope. "I had hoped this would come," she said, opening the letter. "Would you like to see a picture?"

Megan held her breath as Helen pulled a photograph free of its paper clip and passed it across the desk. Dave reached for the picture first, but he leaned over and held it in front of Megan's eyes.

The child was simply beautiful. Fair-skinned, with dark black hair that stood up like a Mohawk in the center of her head. Chubby and healthy-looking, her little belly strained at the seams of a sleeveless sun suit. Someone had propped up in a little painted chair, and a place card beside her leg read *Danielle Li Wingfield*.

Megan swallowed hard and bit back tears.

"Your friends," Helen said, her eyes scanning the letter, "have listed the child with the Southern Child Welfare Agency, our partner in Seoul. They are serving as her foster parents, and the people at Southern are handling the child's paperwork. Everything seems to be in order."

Megan could scarcely tear her gaze from the picture.

Never again would her imagination conjure up faceless images of infants; her child had a name and a beautiful, round-cheeked face!

She reached out and touched the photo. From across the miles, a little piece of her daughter had come home.

"If I were you," Helen said, glancing at her watch, "I'd head straight down to the Immigration office. The lines there can be terribly long, and we can't bring her over until you've done all the INS requires."

Megan clutched her folder to her chest. "We'll go now."

Helen smiled and held out her hand. "I'm sorry, but I need the photo for the file. Would you like me to make you a copy?"

Megan would have nodded, but Dave returned the picture and stood. "Thank you, Ms. Gresham, but our friends in Korea are sending a packet of pictures. They're probably waiting at home."

After thanking Helen and taking one last look at her daughter, Megan hurried after him.


They reached the INS office at one o'clock. Megan took one glance at the crowd occupying every available chair and bench, then took a number from the dispenser on the wall. Their number was 409. The digital readout above the main desk told her they were assisting whoever held number 335.

"I think we have time to get lunch," Dave said, his voice dry. "It's going to be a while."

Megan waved to catch the attention of a uniformed staffer walking by. "Is it always like this?"

The woman didn't bat an eye. "Immigration? We're the busiest office in the district."

Reluctantly, Megan agreed lunch was a good idea, but she insisted they go someplace with quick food. After walking about two blocks, they found a little mom and pop joint and ordered hamburgers and fries. After wolfing down one of the biggest burgers Megan had ever seen in her life, she took

Dave's hand and dragged him back to the INS office. The clock said one-thirty; the digital counter had moved forward to number 350.

Torn between relief that they'd made it back in time and consternation at the slow pace, Megan settled into a worn wooden chair. If she'd known the afternoon would turn into a marathon waiting session, she'd have brought a magazine or book. Then again, she thought, studying the assorted people in the waiting area, she probably would be too distracted to concentrate.

Amazing, the number and variety of people that came to America. Waiting with her were women in Indian saris, men in suits, babies tied in slings around their mother's necks. Like her, each of them clutched a folder of documents and the tiny rip-off number, a ticket to hope and the chance for a new life.

As the afternoon wore on, Megan found herself feeling rusty and frustrated again. She frowned as she glanced at the clock. She had no reason to rush back to Alta Vista, but surely the INS office closed at four-thirty or five. What would she and Dave do if they didn't see someone today? They had planned to drive home tonight, so they didn't have a hotel room or even a change of clothes . . .

At three-thirty, a uniformed woman stood at the main desk and called, "Four-oh-nine?"

Megan leapt to her feet, half-pulling Dave with her. "That's us," she called, hurrying forward. The woman didn't crack a smile, but pointed them toward another caseworker at a desk.

Megan and Dave walked over, introduced themselves to the stern-faced woman working there, then Megan slid the folder with their paperwork across the desk. She briefly explained their situation, told the woman about the baby, and assured her that the adoption was proceeding without a hitch. "Of course, we understand that we have to clear her coming to the United States," Megan said, sinking slowly into the chair before the woman's desk. She gestured toward the folder. "So you'll find everything you need there. Our marriage license, birth certificates, copies of our drivers' licenses—"

The woman peered into the folder, flipped through the pages, then snapped it shut. "I'm sorry, but you've missed the fingerprint office. Immigration law requires us to run your fingerprints through the FBI database before you can apply for permission to bring an alien into the United States."

Megan felt her stomach drop. "We have to be *fingerprinted?* Before we can do any anything else?"

The woman's mouth softened slightly. "If you hurry, you might be able to catch the guy across the street. He does fingerprints—for a fee."

Dave didn't hesitate. He was out of his chair before Megan could respond, so she stood and hurried after him, pausing only long enough to retrieve their precious paperwork from the caseworker's hand.

The "guy across the street" turned out to be a gruff-voiced older fellow who listened to their frantic story with a gentle smile. Megan knew she was making little sense, but he seemed to listen intently as he pressed each of their fingers onto an inkpad, then expertly rolled them across a preprinted card.

When the cards were done, he pulled a stub of a cigar out of his mouth, then smiled and handed the forms to Megan. "Good luck," he said, grinning at Dave. "Now hurry back over there so you can bring that baby home."

Approaching the INS office, Megan felt her heart stop when she saw a rope stretched across the entrance to the INS waiting room. Had the office closed? As they hurried closer, however, she could see people in the reception area beyond. She could have fallen to her knees in gratitude when she realized they had merely stopped taking new arrivals in order to handle those who were still waiting.

The INS staffer at the main desk recognized them immediately. "You won't have to wait again," she promised, glancing toward the caseworker who had spoken to them earlier. "Marcy's ready for you."

With an air of accomplishment, Megan strode over and returned her folder, now complete with fingerprint cards. The caseworker glanced at the documents, stamped their application, then looked up and smiled. "Glad you made it back," she said, standing. "Now if you will both raise your right hands and repeat after me."

Megan had never felt more solemn than in that unexpected moment. Together she and Dave took an oath to protect the child they had petitioned to bring into the United States, then the caseworker handed Megan a sheet of paper. "Go home, fill this in, and return it with a check for the application fee," she said, her tone cool and professional. But her eyes sparkled as she whispered, "And God bless you."

Megan's heart swelled with gratitude as she accepted the application. Everything was falling into place. Step by step, God was bringing them closer to their baby.

They found the first packet of photographs in the mailbox when they arrived home. Though she was dead tired from the trip to Washington, Megan tore open the envelope, then stared at the first picture with unabashed delight. The tiny black and white snapshot in Helen Gresham's office hadn't done Danielle justice—this baby was *adorable*.

Joe and Susan had taken and developed an entire roll of film—shots of the baby having a bath, wet-haired and big-eyed in the plastic tub, shots of her leaning out of a stroller, shots of her on Susan's hip. In one picture, Danielle had been propped against pillows and was falling over, her mouth open in what Megan was certain must have been a belly laugh. A deep dimple adorned her left cheek, a glorious smile lit her face, and, Megan realized as she memorized the photos, the robust baby was no frail infant.

Megan made a mental note to exchange some garments she'd bought earlier in a rush of excitement. This kid was growing like a weed.

"Come home soon," she whispered, pressing the photos

to her chest. "Come home before you outgrow everything in your closet!"

After she and Dave studied every single picture, Megan separated several photos and slipped them into envelopes for Dave's sister, her mother, and her mother-in-law. She set one photo, her favorite, aside for the birth announcement. Tomorrow she'd take it to the drug store and have a zillion reprints made.

"I cannot wait to hold her and love her," she whispered to Dave as they sat on the sofa and drank in the details of the remaining snapshots.

"This little doll will come soon enough," Dave answered, placing his hand on her hair. "All in God's time."

# EIGHT

A strong sense of purpose carried Megan through the next few days. Before Joe Hogan's call, she had existed in a stagnant pool of possibilities; now she felt she and Dave had finally begun to make progress—or, in the words of Samuel Johnson, their sorrow was being lessened by "exercise and motion." The baby God intended for them was waiting in South Korea, and Megan was determined to do all she could to insure that the time of waiting was as brief as possible.

With great regret, on the first Monday in August she knocked on Dr. Duncan's door and gave her notice. She would quit work in two weeks, she told him, because her baby would soon be home. Though they didn't yet have an exact arrival date, they expected her to arrive in less than six weeks—by the end of September, at the latest.

"And I have so much to do," Megan explained, spreading her hands. "I have to shop, and there is paperwork yet to be done, and I've got a lot of reading to catch up on. My baby is three months old, and I need to know what to expect at this age."

The doctor's blue eyes twinkled behind his glasses. "I know I should offer my congratulations," he said, crossing his arms, "but it won't be easy to replace you. Are you sure I can't talk you in to coming back to work after you've had some time to adjust?"

Megan shook her head. "Thank you, sir, but no. I've worked so hard to be a mother, and waited so long . . . I don't want to miss a minute of the experience. And my daughter will need me, so I want to be with her every minute I can."

Dr. Duncan's mouth drooped in a one-sided smile. "I think this is one lucky baby."

Megan shook off the compliment and returned to the desk, then pulled her pocket-sized calendar from her purse and marked off another day. It was August 1—little Danielle had been born on the ninth of April, so she was almost four months old.

Megan sighed. Infancy flew by so quickly! Susan had said Danielle was already a big baby, so if she didn't come home soon Megan might never know what it felt like to hold an infant in her arms . . .

She shook off the thought. She would harbor no regrets, for God had obviously brought this child to them in His timing and for His reasons.

Her eyes fell upon a calendar date marked with a red circle—the day for Helen Gresham's home visit. Korean regulations required the U.S. placement agency to visit the couple's home at least once, so Helen would have to fly to Alta Vista. Megan felt certain the visit would be uneventful— they liked Helen from the moment of meeting her, and Belinda Bishop had already approved their home. So this would be a perfunctory meeting.

Megan looked up and smiled as Mrs. Leber came through the veterinary clinic door, her arms filled with a wicker basket in which a new passel of puppies scrambled upward. "Mrs. Leber," she called, grinning. "Has that Chihuahua been visiting your yard again?"


Dave lowered himself to the sofa and bit his lip as he heard Megan singing in the kitchen. She'd been talkative and excited all through dinner, telling him about Dr. Duncan and what he'd said when she told him she planned to leave in two weeks. From that topic she bounced to the news that his sister in New Orleans had promised to send a box of baby clothes her daughter had outgrown. She'd mailed it a couple of days ago, and the package would arrive at any time.

"I think there are a lot of people who really feel involved with us," Megan had told him, her eyes shining. "Most of these people have been waiting and praying with us for years. I know it sounds silly, because nearly every baby is loved and anticipated, but I can't help feeling that ours has been more anticipated than most. Well—anticipated *longer* than most, in any case."

Dave had let her chatter and ramble, remembering to nod and smile in all the right places, but he breathed a sigh of relief when dinner ended and she rose to stack their plates and do the dishes. He emptied the garbage, fulfilling his part of the dinner deal, then moved to the living room and picked up the newspaper.

But he couldn't concentrate on the articles before his eyes. He couldn't think about anything but the trouble looming over his school.

He had chosen not to teach during this summer break for two reasons—he wanted to be free if they got a baby, and he wanted to be available if he was named to fill the vacancy created by Dr. Comfort's retirement. Though the start of the new school year was only three weeks away, the school board had not yet made any official appointments. They were meeting throughout the week, and things were supposed to be settled soon.

But how? The question nagged at him.

That afternoon he'd heard rumors that the recently commissioned demographic report indicated a shrinking elementary student population in the area zoned for Valley View—and every teacher on staff knew what that dire news could mean. Their school was one of the older campuses in the state, and the land was valuable and situated near a residential area. Even at this late date, the school board might shut Valley View down and sent students elsewhere. If they did, over forty faculty members and administrators would be out of a job.

He lowered the paper to his chest as he stared out the front window. Ordinarily, he'd have shared this news with

Megan the moment he returned home, but he couldn't bring himself to cloud her happiness with dark possibilities. This was one of those 50/50 situations—the school board could close the school, or they could keep it open, and life would continue without a ripple. Why should he worry Megan with desperate situations that *might* be?

The phone rang, and Megan called from the kitchen. "Could you get that, hon? My hands are soapy."

With a sense of foreboding, Dave picked up the phone. "Hello?"

"Mr. Wingfield, this is Helen Gresham. I'm afraid I have a bit of bad news."

Dave sat silently, letting the words drop into his consciousness. Bad news on top of bad news meant more to keep from Megan.

"What is it?" he asked, his voice hoarse.

"It's a bit complicated," Helen said, "but I'll do my best to explain. In Korea, you see, a child cannot be declared abandoned if he or she has been entered into a family register—it's a bit like our birth certificates, only more involved. If a family claims a child, obviously, the child is not abandoned."

"But," Dave lowered his voice in case Megan was listening, "she was left on a doorstep. That's abandonment."

"Not necessarily. The extended family structure in Korea, you see, is more emphasized than in the U.S. And if this child is registered with a family, she is not legally available for adoption."

Dave's breath came raggedly. "But she's not with a Korean family. She's with my wife's friends."

"I know, Mr. Wingfield, but I'm telling you the facts. I'm still planning on visiting you, but I may bring news that you'll have to consider another child."

Helen Gresham's words echoed in his consciousness long after he hung up the phone. He sat on the sofa, trembling with frustration and fear, then flinched when Megan stepped into the room.

"Who was on the phone, hon?""

Dave looked at her, met her gaze, and saw her expression shift from curiosity to apprehension. He couldn't hide this from her—the baby, this *particular* baby, was all she thought about these days.

Drawing a deep breath, he relayed Helen's message as simply as he could. Megan sat on the sofa next to him, her face blank, her eyes expressionless as she stared into space.

"I have to believe this is only a test," she finally said, her voice vacant and hollow. "We have a choice—we can be distracted, disillusioned, and defeated, or we can press on in the faith that Joe and Susan are keeping *our* baby."

She turned and looked at him. "Do you agree?"

Wordlessly, Dave nodded.

Standing, Megan squared her shoulders, then lifted her purse from the table by the door. "I'm going to that little second-hand furniture store by the church. I saw a crib there the other day, and I figure now's as good a time as any to buy it."

She pulled her keys from her handbag. "I'll stop by the hardware store, too, for some paint and a paintbrush. I think I'll paint everything white. It won't be beautiful furniture, but it'll look clean and nice. After all, she's a baby. It's not like she'll know the difference between second-hand and Ethan Allan."

With a little wave in his direction, Megan opened the door and stepped out into the night.

Dave felt his heart twist as he watched her go. In the face of overwhelming odds, his wife would fight the world with faith and a paintbrush.


At work the next morning, Megan greeted owners and handled patients with an almost robot-like precision. Laurie remained quiet and aloof, almost as if she sensed that something was wrong. Dr. Duncan spent most of the morning in surgery, so his thoughts remained elsewhere.

"I will pray and trust," Megan told herself for the hundredth time as she checked the water bowls in the kennels. "God is in control of this situation, and He will walk me through it."

But the moment she shifted her thoughts from that comforting mantra, she felt like Peter sinking into the sea. How could this latest problem possibly work itself out? Dave said that Helen thought they could get another child if Danielle didn't work out, but that option felt wrong somehow. At the INS office, they had applied for *Danielle's* visa, they had listed her name on the application, they had sworn, in their hearts at least, to protect and provide for *her.* How could they pop another child into that particular place in their hearts? They might as well forget about Korea and continue waiting on Belinda Bishop's computers . . .

That thought sent another realization zinging through Megan's brain. Last week, right after their return from Washington, they had gone to the bank and applied for a second mortgage. The banker had frowned at their completed application, particularly when Megan confessed that she would not be working when the baby arrived. The banker had said he'd see what they could do. This adoption would cost over $7,000—money they didn't have in cash, but they could borrow from the equity invested in their home. Most of that amount would go to the Korean agency to cover administrative fees and the baby's airfare; another portion would go to Welcome Home for expenses.

Megan checked the last kennel, then leaned against the wall and crossed her arms. What if they got the loan and couldn't get Danielle? She'd been so convinced Danielle was the child for them that she hadn't worried about getting the loan. After all, Dave had a good job, and they'd been living in their house for three years. The house had been a bargain when they bought it, and they'd made improvements, finishing a room in the basement and adding a back porch . . .

She closed her eyes, remembering how she had cringed at the thought of those adoption fees when they first investigated international adoption. Back then, she could not imagine how they could possibly consider such a notion, now a second mortgage not only seemed wise, but practical. All they needed was the bank's approval, and money would no longer be an issue.

The phone rang, jangling her nerves. Megan's heart skipped a beat when Laurie answered, then put the caller on hold and held the receiver toward Megan. "It's for you," she said simply.

Megan felt her mouth go dry. Laurie knew Dave's voice and would have identified him. Megan's mother never called at work, so this *could* be Belinda Bishop . . .

She licked her dry lips, then took the phone. "Hello?"

"Megan?" Helen Gresham's dignified voice rang in her ears. "I have good news. First, I wanted to tell you that my plane will land at ten a.m. on Monday the fifteenth. I'm excited about our visit. Second, I wanted you to know that everything has been settled in Korea." She chuckled. "Your friend is something else. Apparently he personally carried the baby to the mayor's office in Seoul and made an impassioned plea on your behalf. I'm not certain of the details, but we've just heard from our Korean affiliate. The baby has been cleared. Danielle will be on her way home in about a month, as soon as her paperwork arrives."

Megan pressed her hand to her chest. This news came too suddenly, she couldn't take it in all at once.

She turned and grinned at Laurie. "That's wonderful news, Helen! Dave will be so happy to hear it!"

"I'm pleased it all worked out. So—you'll meet me at the airport on the fifteenth?"

"We'll be there." Megan exhaled a long sigh of relief. "You can count on us."

# NINE

Dave let the car door close with a heavy thud, then picked up his briefcase and trudged toward the door. Of all the moments in this long, exhausting day, the one he dreaded most still lay ahead. Megan had left him a message with the good news about the baby's paperwork, but now he had to counter that joyful announcement with news of his own.

The bad tidings had reached him an hour earlier: Valley View Elementary School would not operate in the next school year. Dave would not be a principal, and he'd be lucky to find an administrative opening in any of the other city schools. That meant he'd be back in the classroom, working for a teacher's salary, and starting over in a new school with new challenges.

Or . . . he and Megan could move. Roanoke, a good-sized city about an hour away, was growing, and he could commute until the house sold. And he'd heard that North Carolina schools districts desperately needed experienced administrators on the elementary level. But if they left the state of Virginia, they'd be out of Belinda Bishop's jurisdiction . . . and Helen Gresham's. He and Megan would have to start the adoption process all over again.

He hesitated before the front door, his hand on the knob. How could he soften this blow? Megan had endured so much already, it hardly seemed fair to ask her to roll with another punch. Any other woman would have already resorted to screaming fits, and many other wives would have thrown up their hands and walked out of the marriage.

He had married a strong woman . . . but even Megan's

strength had limits. He wasn't sure she could handle this latest development, especially when he pointed out that it wasn't fair to ask Danielle to wait.

That little girl deserved a home and loving parents. Joe and Susan Hogan had been the personification of Christian love and faithfulness, but they couldn't keep the child forever. Joe faced the demands of his ministry and family; Susan had her work and three children of her own.

He and Megan would have to let Danielle go to another couple. It should be a simple matter—she had been successfully entered into the system, both in Korea and in the United States. Helen Gresham had other waiting families; one of them, Dave knew, would be thrilled to love Danielle.

Because after the final school board meeting tomorrow morning, Dave would probably not have a job. And the bank would not grant a loan to a couple when neither of them worked, no matter how unique the circumstances.


Megan stepped back and surveyed her gleaming table. In honor of Helen's good news, she had slipped away from work early and prepared a glorious feast—baked chicken with cranberry sauce, broccoli and cheese, golden yeast rolls, and pumpkin pie. If it looked a little like a Thanksgiving dinner, well, tonight they had a lot to be thankful for.

She pulled the crystal candleholders from the china hutch and straightened the tall candle that leaned precariously to the right. After fumbling in the junk drawer for a moment, she found a book of matches and lit the elegant tapers.

She heard Dave's key in the door as she shook the flame off the match. She stepped back and dimmed the kitchen lights, loving the way the candles danced in the semi-darkness. Dave might think she had lost her mind, and he'd be half right. She felt like a completely different person, as if she'd gone from being Megan Wingfield, wife, to Megan Wingfield, mother, in the space of a single afternoon.

She ducked behind a corner as she heard Dave's

approaching footsteps. He seemed to hesitate in the kitchen doorway. "Meg?"

"Welcome home!" She peeked out from behind the corner and grinned, then stepped forward and wrapped her arms about his neck. Impulsively, she kissed him, then lowered her head to the space between his chest and chin. "Can you believe our good news?" she whispered, hearing his heartbeat beneath the soft cotton of his shirt.

"Meg." His hoarse voice was edged with a note of desolation. Alarmed, Meg pulled away and looked at him, reading the grief and despair on his face.

"What's wrong?"

He gestured toward the sparkling table. "Maybe we should sit down."

Moving woodenly, Megan slipped into her chair and sat erect as Dave stared at the burning candles. For a long moment neither said anything, then he drew a deep breath and reported on the latest school board decisions—Valley View would not open this month, the students would be transferred, there were few administrative openings in the city schools. At a meeting tomorrow, the board would decide who would be transferred to what schools; and those for whom there were no jobs would have to find employment elsewhere.

Megan silently watched her husband, who seemed to be wearing his face like a mask. In a passionless voice, he said he could look for work in Roanoke, which meant they'd have to sell the house, or he could find work in North Carolina. But if they moved out of state there would be no adoption.

"Or," his eyes finally met hers, "I could stay here and find work, any kind of work, that would pay the bills until after we get the baby. I don't know if the bank would give us the loan, and I don't know how we could raise thousands of dollars without a bank loan, but I'm willing to try anything. I could deliver newspapers in the morning, and maybe tutor kids in the evenings. I could stay home with the baby if you want to ask Dr. Duncan if he would let you keep your job. I'll do anything you want, but right now I'm too tired and too confused to know what we're *supposed* to do."

Megan stared, her mind and body benumbed, as a tear slowly found its way down her husband's cheek. Her own body quaked with repressed feeling, but she would not weep. Not now. They could not weep together; that would feel like surrender. One of them had to remain strong while the other weakened, one of them had to keep fighting . . . for Danielle.

"Honey," her trembling hand reached out to cover his, "we'll know. Somehow, at some point, the Lord will show us what to do."

Dave swiped away the wetness on his cheek, then drew a deep breath. "As I see it, we have two immediate options."

"And they are?"

"Either stay where we are and pursue Danielle's adoption as far as we can, or we call Helen Gresham and tell her to give the baby to someone else. We can always wait on Belinda Bishop's list. As long as we remain in the state, we'll have a spot there."

His words hit Megan with the force of a physical blow. She closed her eyes. "I don't know what will happen with your job, but I can't lose Danielle. I *won't* lose her, Dave. I'll work, and you'll work, and we'll beg and borrow if we have to. But I can't give up my baby!"

They lay in bed that night without speaking, each of them tossing and turning until the clock struck two. When Dave finally settled and his breathing deepened, Megan sat up in the darkness and looked at his shadowy form.

Men dealt with emotions differently, she knew, yet she couldn't deny that he loved Danielle as much as she did. He would sacrifice everything he possessed if she were their daughter, and in that lay the problem—she *wasn't* their daughter, not yet.

Did God bring that little girl into their lives, or was her arrival mere happenstance? Was it God's will that they expend every effort to bring that particular child into their home, or were they pasting a "God's will" sign on coincidence and foolishly following an expensive dream?

Megan knew some folks in her church would frown on their bank loan. Oh, they wouldn't mind borrowing to buy a house or even a car, but they'd find a second mortgage unspiritual. "If God wanted you to have that baby," she could almost hear them saying, "He'd have provided the finances, too. You should walk away from any situation that will put you in debt."

But Megan felt God *had* supplied the finances—through the possibility of a second mortgage. After all, they were borrowing from the equity in their home, which God had generously provided.

She threw off the light blanket that covered her, then hugged her knees. How could she be certain she'd found God's will? As a child, she had relied heavily upon her parents for guidance, knowing that the biblical command "honor your father and mother" resulted in blessing. Even in college, when her parents tried to encourage her to make her own decisions, she had begged to know their preferences in difficult situations.

As a wife, she believed God often spoke through her husband. Dave trusted her to make most decisions regarding the household, but in important matters she always sought his opinion. In rare situations where they didn't agree, Megan always shared her feelings and convictions, knowing that Dave would respect them even if he decided to follow his own inclinations.

But how were they to decide what to do about Danielle? They had witnessed so many little miracles—Joe's unexpected and unsolicited phone call, the INS paperwork falling into place, and answered prayers regarding Danielle's family registry and availability. Surely the hand of God had manipulated those situations! So how could He now lead them away from this child?

Too burdened to sleep, she slipped out of bed and padded

down the hall and into the baby's room. The freshly-painted crib sat against the far wall, gleaming in the light from the streetlamp outside the windows. Her old bureau, also awash in a fresh coat of paint, stood next to the crib. Adjacent to that stood a bookcase she had discovered in another secondhand furniture store. With a new fabric cover and three inches of foam padding, the bookcase made a perfect changing table, with room for baby wipes and diapers on the shelves beneath.

Shivering in a draft from the air conditioning, Megan rubbed her hands over her arms, then sank to the carpeted floor. She had planned to put a bentwood rocker in this corner. On many a recent night she had soothed her anxious heart to sleep by imagining herself rocking Danielle and reading the soothing cadences of nursery rhymes and *Goodnight, Moon*.

The thought now made her throat ache.

Rubbing her arms again, she glanced at the dark shape at her right hand, then recognized it—the box from Dave's sister, Vicki. Upon hearing the good news about Danielle, she had cleaned out her attic and boxed up all of her daughter's baby things.

Reluctantly, Megan lifted the cardboard flaps. A note lay on top, illegible in the semi-darkness, so she dropped it to the floor. Then her fingers parted tissue paper and pulled out a beautiful smocked dress with lace at the hem and sleeves. The lovely little white dress seemed to glow in the silence of the empty room.

A new anguish seared her heart. What should she do with this box of beautiful things? Keep it in the hope that all would be well, or send it back with a thank you note and regrets?

Her throat tightened, and it was only when she tasted the salt of tears did she realize she was weeping. "Lord," she whispered, her gaze lifting to the silent night outside the window. "What are you asking of me?"

The answer came, slowly and surely, on the wings of

lessons learned in a lifetime of Sunday school. *Jesus asks us only to follow Him . . . to be obedient.*

"Obedient?" she choked on the word. "I would obey, really I would, if I knew what You wanted me to do. I want this baby, and I think You want me to have her. If You want me to give her up, You're going to have to show me clearly." She lifted her chin. "It wouldn't be easy, but we could do it.

*Follow me.*

"Follow You *where?* Follow You *how?*"

As Megan battled her raging emotions in the silence, a realization began to take shape and form: in all the winding length of her life, God had never failed to guide her. She had accepted Jesus as a child, and, like a loving Friend, He had never left her alone or without direction. And when she wanted to turn inward and selfishly dwell on her own hurts, time after time He reminded her . . . that others were hurting, too.

Closing her eyes, she thought for the first time about the others who might be lifting prayers for wisdom at that same hour. Valley View Elementary had employed over forty faculty members, and tonight many of them were walking the floor, as fearful as she about what tomorrow might bring. In Korea, Joe and Susan were caring for *four* children and probably praying that Danielle's adoption would be finalized soon. And in the room next door, a good man slumbered uneasily, burdened with guilt for bringing bad news home to the wife he loved.

"Forgive me, Father." Megan bowed her head as the enormity of her self-centeredness struck her. "I want what You want. I trust Your guiding hand. I praise You for Your goodness to me, even when that goodness takes the form of something I can't understand."

A praise song from church filled her heart, and she found herself paraphrasing the words in a broken whisper: "I will praise You, knowing that my praise will cost me every dream I have ever dreamed."

*Danielle and the future and my motherhood. I said I would not lose her, Lord, but I will let her go, if that's what obedience requires.*

"I will praise You with the joy that comes from knowing I have held nothing back."

*not these baby clothes, not this nursery, not my future*

"I will praise You, for I know nothing can harm me."

*everything comes to me through Your sheltering hand, so I know I can trust You.*

"I will praise You for giving me this opportunity to realize how much I need You."

*I need you for strength to face tomorrow and the day after that. I am at the end of myself, and I've nowhere to turn but to You, Lord.*

"I will praise You for this opportunity to realize Your great provision and loving care."

*You can and will provide . . . if not today, then tomorrow*

"I will praise You for the plan You always reveal in Your time. I will praise You for giving me a husband who loves me. And I will praise You for knowing my mother's heart."

*and for designing it that way*

The next words hurt Megan's throat, but she forced them out into the quiet darkness of the nursery: "Though it costs me everything, I will offer up the sacrifice of praise."

# TEN

Megan woke the next morning to the light touch of sunlight upon her cheek. Momentarily confused by her surroundings, she pushed herself off the carpet. She'd fallen asleep in the nursery, in the midst of baby clothes and the ashes of her dreams . . . desires which now lay in the hands of her heavenly Father.

She staggered into the hall bathroom and stared at her reflection. The nap of the carpet had mottled her cheek; the hair at the top of her head stood upright in some sort of Mohawk imitation, and her eyes were still red-rimmed from weeping.

"Sleeping beauty, indeed," she murmured, turning the faucet. She splashed her face with several bracing handfuls of cold water, then reached for a thick towel on the rack. The singing of pipes in the walls assured her Dave was awake and in the shower. He could probably use a strong cup of coffee.

She walked to the kitchen, plugged in the coffee maker, then cracked open the front door and shot a furtive glance up and down the street. When she was confident there were no neighbors about, she dashed out in her pajamas and picked up the newspaper, then took it to the kitchen.

Dave joined her a few moments later, his hair slicked back and shiny with wet. He wore a long-sleeved shirt, a dark blue tie, and matching navy pants. The conservative look, suitable for an educator eager to impress.

He lifted a brow when he saw her sitting at the table with a cup of coffee. "I saw that you were up already, but making coffee? What's gotten into you?"

She shrugged. "I just wanted to help get your day get off to a good start. Figured a cup of coffee and the paper couldn't hurt."

He sat down beside her, sipped the coffee, and smiled in appreciation. "Perfect, Meg."

"Thanks." She nodded slowly. "That's what I wanted to tell you this morning. Whatever happens in your meeting today, I know things are going to be perfect. We want what God wants and we're committed to Him. So I know things will work out."

He looked at her, a question in his eyes.

She lowered her coffee cup and met his gaze. "Last night I couldn't sleep, so I went into the baby's room to sort of argue my case before God. And I realized that what I said yesterday about nothing being able to give Danielle up—well, I was being stubborn. So, before I finally went to sleep, I gave her to the Lord. He loves that baby even more than I do, and I know He wants what's best for her. So whether she comes home to our house or someone else's, I'm okay. I want what God wants, no matter what that is."

Dave's eyes burned with the clear, deep blue that burns in the heart of a flame, then he reached out and gently stroked her cheek. "I love you," he whispered, gratitude gleaming in his eyes.

His hand pulled her forward until they met forehead-to-forehead. "Father, we are Yours," he prayed, his hand warm against the back of her neck. "Work Your will through us today, and we will give You the power, and honor, and glory for whatever comes. In the name of Jesus we ask these things."

When Megan lifted her head, Dave's eyes shone with confidence. She smiled, knowing that no matter what happened in the school board meeting, Mr. and Mrs. Dave Wingfield would be at peace.

Later that morning, Megan moved through her usual

routines of attending patients, assisting Dr. Duncan, and helping Laurie at the desk. She functioned automatically, only half-thinking about her actions, while her brain wrestled with the idea of revoking her resignation. She had another week and half before her resignation at the clinic became final . . . but what if she'd made a terrible mistake?

If Dave lost his job, she certainly couldn't afford to leave hers. Dr. Duncan would almost certainly love to keep her, but he had already begun to interview prospective veterinary technicians. In fact, if Laurie's scribbled notation on the calendar could be trusted, Megan was fairly certain he had already had asked someone to report next week to begin training for her position.

Begging to keep her job at this late date would be unfair to Dr. Duncan and to whomever he planned to hire. So she couldn't change her mind about leaving.

She bit her lip. If the news from today's school board meeting was as bad as they feared, she could always apply at another veterinary office in town, though that would seem disloyal to Dr. Duncan. Or she could set aside her training and investigate a new line of work—pet sitting, dog walking, or perhaps pet grooming. She knew nothing about how to give fancy hair cuts to poodles and Malteses, but she could wash a dog as well as anyone. The world of dog shows had always interested her—she'd have to be trained, of course, but if she wormed her way into the circle of professional handlers who worked the dog show circuit, she could make a tidy sum working weekends and summers . . .

She shook those thoughts away. She wouldn't worry. She would take one day at a time and wait to see what God would do. He was in control; He owned the entire situation. Surrendering her dreams and her child had been the most difficult act of her life, but she had done it. Now she couldn't—*wouldn't*—take those things back.

Her thoughts filtered back to the day when they had first learned there would be no biological babies. Dr. Comfort had stood in her kitchen and given her a promise: "Hope deferred makes the heart sick, but when the desire comes, it is a tree of life."

When would her tree of life bloom?

"Hey, Meg," Laurie called from the reception desk. "Take a look at what's coming our way."

Megan stood from her chair behind the filing cabinet and looked out the glass door. Instead of the pet owner and patient she expected, she saw a man approaching, his arms overflowing with yellow roses.

The flowers drooped as the man struggled to free his arm and open the door, and that's when Megan saw his face. This was no florist or delivery person—it was her husband.

Without a word, Megan rounded the corner of the desk and flew to the door, nearly tripping over a Weimaraner stretched out across the tile floor. "Dave," she cried, coming to an abrupt halt in front of him. Strangled by a sudden rise of hopes and fears, she could scarcely breathe. "What's happened?"

The yellow blossoms tilted to one side, and Dave's lopsided grin appeared. "You're looking at the new assistant principle of Pleasant Hill Elementary," he said, stepping forward to place the bundle of roses in her arms. "I received the appointment this morning. It's the same job I had at Valley View, and at the same salary. It's not a promotion, but—"

"It's perfect." Megan threw her free arm around his neck. As the people in the waiting room looked on in amusement, she planted a loud, smacky kiss on his smiling mouth.

"We're okay," he whispered, holding her close. "We still have a job."

*We still have a baby.*

"Thank you," she whispered, closing her eyes as her thoughts lifted to the One who had made it all possible. "Thank you, Jesus."

One month after their visit to Washington, Megan called

the Welcome Home office in Washington to check on the progress of their case. Helen reported that Danielle's paperwork had not yet arrived from Korea, but they were confident the documents would arrive soon.

Megan hung up, simultaneously frustrated and relieved. The night before she'd draped herself in hope and fortitude and attended a baby shower for her friend, Susie. Susie's baby, a beautiful little boy, sat in the center of the sofa, while another friend, Debbie, bounced her infant daughter on her lap. Not to be outdone, Megan passed pictures of Danielle around the circle. "I'm so sorry your baby isn't here yet," Susie whispered in a private moment, but the words didn't sting like they would have in a few months ago.

"I'm grateful to have pictures," Megan said, handing over a snapshot. "I thank the Lord for these."

On Monday of the next week, the bank called with more good news—the Wingfield's house had appraised for $15,000 over the amount they owed on the mortgage, so they could pick up a check for the $7,000 they needed whenever they could find the time to stop by.

Once the money had been safely deposited in their savings account, Megan paced in her empty house and stared at the calendar. She'd been unemployed for three weeks, and her soul was beginning to feel rusty again. School would begin in one week, so Dave had his hands full with preparation for his new students. She had hoped to be busy mothering her baby by this time, but it looked as though September would arrive without Danielle.

The days melted into weeks as September slid away in a blur of reds and golds. Near the end of the month, Helen Gresham called to ask for Danielle's airfare. "The check will be sent to Korea as soon as the baby's documents arrive here," Helen explained, "then she will be issued a Korean passport. While the passport is being finalized, you can finish filing with the Department of Immigration. Our babies usually arrive about four weeks after the paperwork."

Megan was delighted to have a task to exercise the rust

away, so she hurried to the bank, ordered a certified check, and sent it to Washington by registered mail.

Unfortunately, her task did not take long, and soon she found herself waiting again. Inactivity chafed upon her—like Martha of the New Testament, she had never been happy to sit when she could be working. She consoled herself with the thought that if the documents were due any day, and Danielle would arrive four weeks after her paperwork, she'd probably be arriving sometime in late October . . . perhaps in time for Dave's birthday on the twenty-first.

The days fell, like the autumn leaves on the oak outside her window, one after the other. Megan read books on child care, visited her mother and sister, and tried not to be jealous of Melanie's progressing pregnancy. She did not covet Melanie's baby, but she did resent her sister's *security*. Mel knew where her baby was and approximately when it would be delivered. Megan had no assurances.

One day, when the tedium of waiting grew intolerable, Megan picked up the phone and called her mother. "It's so hard not to want her here now," she said, taking pleasure in the liberty of venting. "Danielle's five month birthday is in two weeks and I could go *crazy* if I think about missing these early months of her life. So I try not to think about it, but it's almost impossible—"

"I wasn't going to tell you this," her mother interrupted, her voice quiet and thoughtful, "but maybe it's something you need to know."

Megan's inner alarm bells rang. "What?"

"Your baby shower. Melanie and I are giving you a shower next week. We wanted it to be a surprise, but it sounds like you could use something to look forward to."

Megan could hardly sleep the night before the shower. And when the last party guest left her mother's house, Megan looked over the mounds of frilly dresses and diapers and books and crib sheets and marveled at the generosity and good wishes of her friends. Then, sighing, she prayed Danielle would have a chance to enjoy their gifts before she outgrew them.

On a gray afternoon, Megan sat in the living room window seat and stared out at the rain drizzling over the driveway. It was the eleventh of October, and they not only did not have their daughter, they still had not heard when she would arrive. Lately Megan hated even to go to church—everyone she knew insisted upon asking when the baby was coming home. Each time she answered, "I don't know" she felt as if she were acknowledging a colossal defeat.

She was trying to be patient. Every day she struggled to silence her fears and doubts. God had done so many things for them—protected them during the job crisis, directed them to a special baby, provided money when they had no means to earn any—so why was He testing their patience? Megan had been waiting three years for a child, and every other expectant mother waited nine months. Why did she deserve such a long-term sentence?

"Sometimes," she told Samson as the cat jumped into her lap, "I think I'll still be sitting here a year from now. Danielle will have outgrown everything in the nursery, and you'll be the only one to play with her toys."

The cat purred, and Megan straightened at the sight of headlights shining through the gray drizzle. The mail carrier had come early, probably in an effort to outrun the rain, and was placing what looked like a letter in her mailbox.

"Be back in a minute, Sam." She dumped the cat off her lap and hurried to the front door, then sprinted through the drizzle. Inside the mailbox, a blue airmail envelope sat atop the catalogs and bills. She pressed the precious packet to her chest in an effort to keep it dry, then ran back into the house.

This letter from Korea did not contain pictures, just an update from Susan. "Joe was hoping to come to Alta Vista and personally escort Danielle home," she had written, "but now it looks like he'll be unable to get away. Danielle is doing well, but she's so attached to me that she screams even when we leave her with a sitter to go to the market."

Megan felt a sharp twist of pain. Danielle should be *home*, attaching to *her*. She felt a sharp pang of jealousy, followed by regret for what Danielle would have to endure in the coming days. The baby would have to leave the loving foster home she'd known and come to America—a tremendous adjustment, even for an infant. Megan's heart ached to think of causing Danielle pain. Babies adapted quickly, the experts said, but how easily could a five-month-old adapt when she was taken from the home she had known half her life?

Desperate for comfort, she picked up her Bible and settled back into the window seat. Flipping through the thin pages, she read her favorite proverb again (not *if* the desire comes, but *when*), then idly turned a few pages back.

Another verse caught her eye, a Psalm:

You keep track of all my sorrows.
You have collected all my tears in your bottle.
You have recorded each one in your book.

As if the verse had called them forth, tears welled in her eyes. God was keeping track of every tear—and she seemed to be weeping buckets these days. She wept at the slightest provocation, even sentimental television commercials and sappy country songs could send her into a crying jag . . .

The ringing of the telephone broke into Megan's thoughts. She carried Susan's letter into the kitchen and stared at it through bleary eyes as she picked up the receiver.

Her heart jumped at the sound of a familiar voice. Helen Gresham was calling from Washington with good news. Danielle's legal documents had finally arrived from Korea, so the agency required only three more items: a letter of approval from the Department of Immigration, a letter from the Virginia state office in Richmond, and Danielle's passport from Korea.

Megan could hear a smile in the social worker's voice as she finished her report: "It should be two weeks at the shortest, three at the longest. She's nearly home."

Tears of joy blurred Megan's vision as she hung up the phone.

On the 26$^{th}$ of October, Helen called again. Danielle was ready, another child was ready, but they were waiting on a third child to be cleared before they would book the children's flight. "Plan on next Tuesday," Helen said. "If there are any changes, I'll let you know. And as soon as I have her flight information, I'll call."

Megan hung up and sent a smile winging across the room. "Tuesday," she told her husband, knowing her smile explained everything. "Seven more days."

Megan filled the long week with busy work—she cleaned the baby's room, scoured out the kitchen cabinets, and organized the clothes in Danielle's closet—the tiny 12-months dresses on the right, followed by the 18-months, then 24-months, and finally a couple of larger dresses she'd been unable to resist in a Polly Flinders outlet. One dress, a red-and-white concoction of tulle and ribbon, hung at the far left, size 6x. Megan looked at the huge dress and shrugged. Danielle would fit into it eventually. Her coming home was truly no longer a matter of *if*, but *when*.

On Saturday evening, Megan's mother called with breathless news. "Melanie just had her baby," she said, yelling to be heard over the commotion in the background. "A boy! She had him at the birthing center, and barely had time to get there before the baby came."

"You should have called me," Megan said, frowning. "I would have liked to be there—and I could have handled it."

"There wasn't time, believe me." Her mother's voice was soothing. "Melanie had the baby quickly. I didn't get here until after it was all over."

"Wow." Megan smiled, drinking in the unexpected wonder. Melanie's due date was November 16, so this little guy had come early . . . and he'd managed to beat his older cousin home by at least three days.

"I'll be over to see her tomorrow," Megan promised, making a mental note to stop by the mall to pick up a gift for a baby boy.

She hung up, knowing she could be happy for her sister without reservation. After all, she was a mother, too, with a baby arriving in seventy-two hours.


On Monday morning, Helen called with concrete details—Danielle would be arriving with four other children, not on Tuesday, but on Friday evening. Megan swallowed her disappointment about the date and consoled herself with the realization that at last they knew a definite date and time: 5:59 p.m., November fourth. Their little girl was finally coming home.

Megan spent the week in domestic activities—she planted tulips, raked the last bedraggled leaves from the lawn, and began a cross-stitched family portrait for her mother, complete with two new babies in the family. On Thursday night she boiled baby bottles, packed a diaper bag with disposables, and tucked in a new outfit, pink booties, and a soft yellow blanket. The car seat and baby stroller waited in the car.

After a leisurely lunch on Friday morning, Dave and Megan got into the car and began to back out the driveway. Another vehicle screeched to a halt in the road behind them, and as Megan turned, she saw Dr. Stella Comfort leaning out the driver's window, waving. "I heard the good news!" she called, her eyes shining. "I'll be praying for you!"

The four-hour drive to Washington National Airport seemed to take forever, and not even the stark beauty of the autumnal countryside could take Megan's mind off her impending motherhood. Washington traffic had shifted into flee-for-the-weekend mode when they hit the Beltway, and after they finally found a parking place at the airport, they had to run and catch a shuttle to the terminal.

Breathless, Dave and Megan reached the gate at 5:30 p.m.,

where they learned that the children's flight had been delayed from 5:59 to 6:33. Helen Gresham stood there, soothing each of the four anxious couples with a calm and gracious smile. Megan wanted to camp out next to Helen's side, but realized she shouldn't be possessive. Each woman in their small circle probably saw Helen as their personal rock of Gibraltar.

She suppressed a smile as she looked around the group. Each couple was as loaded down as she and Dave were, for each expected a child: one, a 21-month-old girl, another a six-month-old boy, and the other a ten-month old girl.

When at last the plane arrived, Megan stood on tiptoe and scanned each face as if by some miracle Danielle might walk herself off the plane. Every single passenger—a seemingly endless stream of them—entered the gate area before Helen and three other Welcome Home social workers boarded the plane to fetch the children. Finally the quartet reappeared and stepped into the blinding light of strobic camera flashes. Helen, the last woman off the plane, carried Danielle.

Megan stared in stupefaction when she recognized the smile she had memorized from precious photographs. Weeping silently, she took the baby from Helen for a brief hug, then handed her to Dave . . . her daddy.

Danielle grinned the entire time. As a few curious spectators drew near, she grinned even more . . . an active, curious little ham.

Megan wasn't sure what impulse guided her actions, but she opened the diaper bag, spread the yellow blanket on the carpet, and gently pulled off Danielle's pajamas and wet diaper. In no time at all she had dressed her baby in a clean diaper, fresh cotton booties, and a soft flannel sleeper.

And as she passed their precious daughter to Dave, she couldn't help noticing that the other families were changing their babies, too. Perhaps, she thought, watching them, the urge to dress these children came from practical considerations—after all, they'd been flying for nearly 24 hours. But Megan believed the urge sprang from deeper instincts. After waiting so long and working so hard, each family wanted to dress the child in clothes *they* had prepared and provided. Somehow, the simple act of placing clean clothes on a baby helped make him yours.

The words from a long-ago afternoon returned on a tide of memory. In the park, Andre's mother had described the experience perfectly: adoption was a time of waiting and a time of hard labor, complete with every pain and every joy. And now that their child had come home, Megan knew she had been blessed.

As Dave cooed and bounced the baby in his arms, Megan gathered the top and bottom of the orange pajamas Danielle had worn on the plane. She'd save these things for her daughter's memory box.

Then her gaze fell upon the crumpled yellow socks she'd peeled from those chubby little feet. They were unlike any booties she'd ever seen—longer than American baby socks, and embroidered with an image of a bumblebee hovering over a blossom.

She laughed softly as she smoothed out the wrinkles. She held a little bit of Korea, a small part of her baby's history, the essence of everything she had dreamed . . . and God had allowed. In the last three years she had been tested, tried, shaped, and hammered. At time she had borne the pain stoically, at other times she had whined and screamed and pounded the floor. But through it all, she had been able to trace God's hand of provision. And that assurance of His abiding faithfulness would get them through the terrible twos, adolescence, dating . . . and the heart-rending moment when they would watch their darling daughter walk into the arms of her future husband.

Megan's throat tightened at the thought.

No one had ever promised that adoption—or parenting—would be easy. Just worthwhile.

She swallowed the lump in her throat, then wrapped the yellow socks in the pajamas and placed the bundle into the diaper bag. "Come on, Dad and daughter," she said, lifting the bag to her shoulder. "Let's go home."

# ABOUT THE AUTHOR

Angela Hunt, who has written over 125 books for children and adults, freely confesses that this is the most autobiographical book she has ever written. "Some of the passages came straight from my journal," she says, "and most came straight from my heart. My husband worked at a church, not a school, and I'm a writer, not a vet tech. But the trials and the feelings . . . they're all true. I lived them."

She and her husband live in Florida and their adopted children, a boy and a girl, are now in their twenties. They also have a lovely little granddaughter who continues to spread the Joy.